Close
to
Home

Happy Birthday Mayur!

What better gift than this? Come home soon.

love, Rahul

12/10/2014

Close to Home

PARVATI SHARMA

zubaan

PENGUIN
VIKING

ZUBAAN
128 B, 1st Floor, Shahpur Jat, New Delhi 110 049, India
in collaboration with

PENGUIN BOOKS
Published by the Penguin Group
Penguin Books India Pvt. Ltd, 7th Floor, Infinity Tower C, DLF Cyber City, Gurgaon 122 002, Haryana, India
Penguin Group (USA) Inc., 375 Hudson Street, New York, New York 10014, USA
Penguin Group (Canada), 90 Eglinton Avenue East, Suite 700, Toronto, Ontario, M4P 2Y3, Canada
Penguin Books Ltd, 80 Strand, London WC2R 0RL, England
Penguin Ireland, 25 St Stephen's Green, Dublin 2, Ireland (a division of Penguin Books Ltd)
Penguin Group (Australia), 707 Collins Street, Melbourne, Victoria 3008, Australia
Penguin Group (NZ), 67 Apollo Drive, Rosedale, Auckland 0632, New Zealand
Penguin Books (South Africa) (Pty) Ltd, Block D, Rosebank Office Park, 181 Jan Smuts Avenue, Parktown North, Johannesburg 2193, South Africa

Penguin Books Ltd, Registered Offices: 80 Strand, London WC2R 0RL, England

First published by Zubaan and Penguin Books India 2014

ISBN 9789383074822

Typeset by Jojy Philip, New Delhi
Printed at Replika Press Pvt. Ltd, India

A PENGUIN RANDOM HOUSE COMPANY

For my mother, who doesn't believe in half-measures
For my father, who believes in books
With lots of love

Contents

1

Sharing a joint isn't falling in love (not even in Jangpura ext.)

If she hadn't met Jahanara at all, Mrinalini would have missed the quite awesome experience of being worshipped. It's a nice thing to be worshipped if, like Mrinalini, you have just begun a desultory search for career in a dotcom of primary colours and grand ambitions that rather outshine your own, and your boyfriend has left to study finance in England leaving you with the implicit promise of a marriage you're not wholly sure you want, but perhaps wouldn't mind, and then your roommate reveals she's gay and begins to woo you in a poetic and doomed kind of way. If, in the process, Jahanara's heart broke, Mrinalini thought you could hardly blame her because it's not like she had even *known* Jahanara was gay or likely to fall in love with her.

Purely practical concerns had brought them together: Mrinalini needed someone to share the rent with, and Jahanara, whom she'd known only kind-of by-the-way in college, wanted to be able to smoke a joint or two of a Sunday afternoon without looking over her shoulder for the sudden influx of a parent. So, Jahanara moved out of what she called her natal home in Maharani Bagh into Mrinalini's two-roomed, three-side-open, door-bangingly breezy barsati in Jangpura Extension.

Mrinalini, never loathe to try a new diversion, acquired the happy habit of sharing Jahanara's marijuana. It was, she agreed, a beautiful thing for hours to pass in peaceably contemplating flocks of pigeons swelling and dispersing against the evening light, or in playing a tape, over and over, letting the music sink into the soft damp breeze that washed monsoon afternoons in grey. By their side they would have bowls of soupy Maggi and crumbling chocolate cake. It was during one such session, in fact, that Jahanara, biting her lip and taking many conversational detours, unveiled her sexuality.

Mrinalini was so obviously delighted by this – the dotcom, though unstinting by way of motivational talk and pizza lunches, offered little real excitement, and Siddhartha only called on Sundays – and so eager with her questions and generous in her felicitations, that Jahanara, who had tensed as if for a blow after uttering the words *I think I'm gay*, had uncoiled and unfurled and unthinkingly discovered, in the time it took them to roll another, that she only ever wanted to tell Mrinalini all her secrets and fears, and that the strength of her feeling being what it was, it must be, it had to be, reciprocated.

So, with trembling heart and flowing hand, Jahanara wrote Mrinalini a letter, a long letter – it covered four pages on both sides – announcing her love, denouncing her fate, and pleading for refuge in Mrinalini's soft eyes.

Mrinalini, having never received avowals of such surrender, was a little troubled, but overall pleased. She went out onto the balcony, where Jahanara was hiding in a corner, her head in her hands, and hugged her friend, who turned and said with an expression of abject sorrow, "I'm sorry!"

"Shh! Don't be sorry."

"I'm so sorry."

"Shh!"

"But I'm…"

But the weather was mild, they were both high, and Mrinalini lightly touched Jahanara's lips with her own. Jahanara, who had never kissed a woman before and hardly dared dream she ever would, froze for a minute before she smiled and, folding her arms around Mrinalini's neck, kissed her back. It was pleasant, maybe even more so, and though no greater intimacy ever ensued between the two girls, Jahanara didn't object. She was happy to be allowed to sit with an arm wrapped loosely around Mrinalini's waist, kissing her shoulder or her neck or her hair as they listened to the lilting repetitions of a thumri or the guttural throat-clearings of a raga or, usually upon Mrinalini's insistence, the nasal dronings of Bob Dylan; and she tried not to mind that Siddhartha still called every Sunday.

It was a habit he'd inherited from his parents who, too, had called him every Sunday that he was away from them, in boarding school and college. To make the call himself, now, gave Siddhartha a peculiar, protective pleasure; he was nothing if not punctilious in the matter of maintaining what they called, with a bashful sense of being quite grown-up, their long-distance relationship.

One such Sunday, the flatmates were drinking tall, half-litre glasses of cold coffee that Mrinalini had woken with a craving for and Jahanara had made: creamy and bitter and frothy on top. Mrinalini had forgotten her heavy black mobile phone in a pool of sweet lemonade the night before and it had ceased to function. Now, it lay in bits and pieces, drying under the fan. Soon enough, Siddhartha would be trying to call; and thinking, perhaps, that his inability to do so was an augury of her own good fortune, Jahanara said, "Tell me, then. What will it be like at our wedding?"

Mrinalini sat up a little, or she slumped a little – she moved, at any rate, so a small breath of air opened between their bodies – and she said, "You'll have to ride a ghodi. That's one thing."

"Really? I didn't know you'd be excited by all that."

"Well yeah, obviously! You'd have to ride a ghodi and we'd have to have a *fabulous* sangeet, and during the lavaan I'd cry a little."

"The lavaan?"

"You know, the pheras – we'd have to do it the Sikh way, wouldn't we? And afterwards, there'd be a lunch and then my doli would leave and then my father would probably cry like anything."

"He would?"

"Oh yes. Highly senti, my father."

"Well, what if I didn't want a Sikh wedding? What if I refused?"

"You'd refuse?" Mrinalini raised one eyebrow. It was a gesture that never ceased to weaken Jahanara, who grinned broadly in response and shook her head: Never.

"But what if my parents refused? What if they said you had to convert?"

"Oh boy. That'd be trouble, then."

"Really?"

"Definitely. My mother'd have a heart attack. She'd go crazy, there's no doubt. My father, I don't know if he'd actually forbid it, but he'd have to take her side, wouldn't he? I mean, I know this – some second-cousin of mine went off and married a Muslim, and *her* parents were okay about it, more or less, but my mother was a sighing-tutting *bomb* waiting to explode. We had a huge fight, she wouldn't let me go for this big birthday party and we didn't talk for a week. And I was fourteen or something. It's not like I was slouching outside some mosque waiting to be picked up."

"Wow," said Jahanara.

"Yeah. I'm sorry – did I not mention earlier, my mother's a fanatic?" Mrinalini squeezed the hand that held hers and laughed.

"What's so funny?"

"Well just. I mean – she doesn't mind *you* at all. She likes you: she sent you all that halwa last month."

Having managed a small laugh of her own in reply, Jahanara changed the subject.

Still, the notion of Mrinalini's mother's communal tendencies bothered Jahanara, who pondered the matter all day before raising it again that evening. Outside, the more elderly of Jangpura's denizens had embarked on pre-dinner shuffles around the neighbourhood, the colony dogs had hauled themselves out from under cars to bark greetings at each other in the cooler air, while young girls and their pre-pubescent brothers played hop-skip-jump games of badminton with fraying shuttlecocks.

"Maybe," said Jahanara, licking a fleck of tobacco from her upper lip, "maybe your mother will change her mind when we have children."

"Yeah," said Mrinalini, in a distracted way, turning the pieces of phone over in her hands, "You mean like in a movie? Good luck with *that*."

"Wait, no. See: in the beginning she'll not speak to you, and call me names and probably not let us into her house – she'll slam the door in our faces –"

"She really will. You shouldn't laugh!"

"And you'll be all weepy and I'll be very noble, and you'll become a famous writer and she'll not even come to your big award ceremony –"

"Yeah, but I'll thank her anyway in my speech –"

"You'll look straight into the camera and say, 'I want to thank my mother, who taught me *love* is *courage*' –"

"But she'll turn off the TV and have a big fight with my father."

"Yeah. But... but *then* one day we'll have this kid, you know. It'll be all squealing and red and you'll be lying exhausted in a hospital and all these people will be calling to congratulate us and I'll say, 'Don't you want to call your parents?'"

"And I'll say, 'My god, no way!'"

"But I'll call them anyway. Or will you? Shall I?"

"Pleasure's all yours, Jahan," Mrinalini picked up the phone battery and shook it.

"Fine, then. I don't mind – I'll only call. Maybe I'll call your father first?"

"Ha! Even I can call my father – he'll probably be there only, sitting next to you."

"Yeah. Maybe I'll just get him to call your mother then?"

"Poor man. He's in enough trouble already. You want him to be the hero of this movie?"

"No no. Accha, okay, I'll only call. Probably she'll hang up on me, though."

"*Probably* she will, yes."

"Then?"

"Then I don't know. It's your movie – I'm just calling for my sedatives."

Jahanara laughed. "Fine then. You know what, nobody'll call her just now because we're too scared, so we'll just send a photo back with your father. And then…"

"Then?" Mrinalini took a glug of water from a plastic bottle on the table and began to reassemble the phone.

"Then, I think, years shall pass."

A bit of plastic slipped from Mrinalini's fingers as she laughed, "*Montage!*"

"Ha. Yeah, exactly like that. What'll happen is, I'll be sitting with the kid – here probably – we'll be sitting with all its toys and playing and your mother –"

"I'm not buying any toys."

"No toys?"

"No. What does it need toys for? They break and get lost and they're very expensive. Kids don't need toys. Just give them a cardboard box and they're happy."

"A cardboard box? What're you saying? Kids *need* toys."

"No they don't. Let them use their imaginations!"

"Fine. Let's not give it any food while we're at it."

Mrinalini laughed as she pressed at the buttons of her phone.

"Show me that?" Jahanara reached for the phone and shook it.

"Obviously they need food. Nobody *needs* toys. Except you, it seems."

"But my god – what's it going to do with one stupid carton?"

"It can have *lots* of cartons. I don't mind."

"Oh wow. All the other kids'll be *so* jealous. They'll all go home and be all, oh Mrinalini aunty's son has so many cartons!"

Mrinalini held her hand out for the dead phone. "It can *make* things with its cartons. It'll be good for its *brain*."

"Yeah. Mrinalini aunty's son gets a whole meal every day. Of tamatar. And kheera. And he's got all these *big* cartons, and *small* cartons –"

"Yeah, and if it doesn't behave, I'll bundle it *into* a carton."

"No doubt. It'll be the most joyful childhood. So okay, fine. I'll be sitting here with one kid hiding from its lunch in its dabba and your mother will be watching from the window. And I'll be telling him, listen it's okay, as soon as you're old enough to run properly, we'll leave this madhouse and we will go to a toy shop and she'll be all – your mother will think, well thank god *one* of them has sense, and she will come in and she will embrace me to her bosom."

"Ha! She'll lock you *both* up in the bathroom is what she'll do."

"No, she won't."

"Yes, she will."

"No, she won't. What, does she not approve of *anything*?"

"No," said Mrinalini and she rose. "She approves of Shakespeare, kind of. But that's it. Accha, I'm going down for a bit, we need detergent."

"Detergent? Now?"

"And I'll get one of those Maggie soups for dinner."

"Accha. I can go if you like? It's hot out."

"No, no. It's fine."

Since it was clear as a blinding June afternoon to anyone except Jahanara that Mrinalini wasn't throwing her eggs into any kind of lesbian basket, ever, Mrinalini hardly thought it necessary to mention that she was also going down to call Siddhartha. Having bought her detergent, and her dehydrated soup, and a half-kilo of sugary green grapes, she stopped at a PCO where, with the whir of a small fan's wings in her ears, she called her parents, and then Siddhartha. When Jahanara heard Mrinalini climb back up the stairs to their barsati, she stopped pacing their two rooms and arranged herself on a cushion, with a magazine open across her face. She looked up when Mrinalini entered, smiled, and rose to help her with her plastic bags.

Still, it had grown dark while Mrinalini was away, and the busy chatter of dinner preparing in other kitchens had given Jahanara a disquieting sense of her own lamp-lit loneliness. That night, there were anxious knots in Jahanara's belly that Mrinalini's febrile cheerfulness wouldn't undo, and they both drank too much cheap whiskey over the evening and argued unhappily but tenaciously about Kashmir to disguise their fidgets and passed out without warning well before 10 o'clock, without dinner and the lights still on.

A few months later, through no fault of hers, Mrinalini's dotcom went bankrupt. Thereafter, Mrinalini could have joined a small but idealistic publishing house, she did contemplate journalism, and she had lunch with an energetic friend in advertising. Eventually though, what happened was that Siddhartha came home and Mrinalini abandoned the idea of regular employment altogether and married him – even if she only put it this way in her blackest moods.

Such moods were rare since Siddhartha wasn't just a caring and sexually adventurous husband, he was also wealthy: his family came from Jor Bagh, even if spiteful intra-familial litigation meant that the house, on the leafiest avenues of central Delhi and worth crores, was crawling with termites. Since none of the contesting parties would themselves exterminate these pests – nor allow another to – it's likely Siddhartha had some premonition of his fortune turning to dust in this game of bitter chicken. With becoming modesty, then,

Siddhartha had flaunted no signs of his privilege in college. The softness of his skin he hid under a straggly beard, his light brown eyes brimmed with a nameless, ahistoric, empathy – particularly when he bought, like everyone else, his cigarettes by the stick and drank cheap, warm beer from the bottle, the cap of which he had learnt to prise open with his teeth. When, one night, Mrinalini sneaked into his room and sucked upon a heady mixture of metal foil and warm fizz, she did not notice the softness of his accent but only his large, careful hands and how certain he was of three things: he loved her, he loved her, he loved her.

Further: Siddhartha was a perfectly respectable 5 foot, 10; tall enough to allow Mrinalini (a reasonable 5 foot 3 herself) to rest her head on his shoulder when they walked – to rest so comfortably, in fact, that she could even sense the beating of his pulse, the gentle flow of his blood rising as if from a great distance.

They fit, they were meant to be, everyone said so; and plus, he asked her.

It was perfect: he'd planned every detail. Afterwards people asked Mrinalini, did she know, did she guess what he was up to? Mrinalini said no, and sometimes she said yes; and most often she said, well, she knew he would… *eventually* – and that drew the most generous laughter.

Siddhartha managed to be both self-deprecating and cocky when he teased her in front of these gathered relatives. "Arre, how could she not know? Eating dinner on a raft in a lagoon. I'd have to be real bhondu if I didn't ask her then."

It was certainly one of the most, no *the*, certainly *the* most beautiful night of their lives. How could it not have been?

They had spent the day snorkelling in the warm, clear-green waters of a resort somewhere along a chain of miniature, white-sanded islands in the Philippines, floating past fish in neon colours, plump and greedy with their open mouths. They had spent the afternoon half dozing, half making love in a light, airy room, its wooden floors dusted with the sand they carried home with them. And at night they had climbed into a motorboat and puttered their way to a deep lagoon, surrounded on three sides by soaring cliffs, a small raft tethered at its centre.

Here, they were handed to a round-faced waiter in white, who sat them at a table laid for two and filled their glasses with champagne before turning on a small two-in-one, which began to pour out a sweet stream of old Hindi film songs.

"I didn't realise how deep it is," Siddhartha said later, "all through dinner, I sat there thinking what if she drops it? That's seventy feet of water and if she tumbles in after and I can't swim – it was *pitch* black and seventy feet, that's no joke."

Still, for dessert he overcame his worry and asked for her love till the end of their days. They danced on the raft, very gently, and Mrinalini wept a little on his shoulder, from the wine and from the music, of course, but also from that fleeting, magical sense of being fully realized. She promised him all the love she would ever conjure and he whispered to her, her soft hair tickling his long nose, "Thank you my baby, my darling, my jamun."

That was his little joke, my janeman, my janam, my jamun, and it made her laugh as she cried in the most perfect way.

* * *

Mrinalini made several attempts to get in touch with Jahanara before the wedding, sending her sentimental emails and formal invitations, but got no response.

Afterwards, she would send her birthday cards by post and text messages on Eid, but Jahanara ignored these overtures, too, in the interest of her convalescent heart, which was all too liable, still, to fall into daydreams of what might have been.

So, for example, Jahanara might be invigilating an exam when the hurried scratching of pens would fade and she'd be on a large bed with a small boy, playing with vrooming plastic cars, perhaps, or big blocks or paper planes,

"Listen!"

"What!"

"When Mama comes to take you to bed today, what'll you say?"

"You say?"

"No. You say?"

"You say?"

"No. You say?"

"*You* say!"

"Okay, okay. You say, 'to SLEEP, to SLEEP, perchance to DREAM'. Okay?"

"No."

"Oh, come on. 'to SLEEP, to SLEEP, perchance to DREAM', okay?"

Mrinalini comes in and raises an eyebrow at the two of them, then all three are in bed and there's a pillow fight and then Jahanara has her in her arms, and then.

Over time, as she began to frequent queer groups and become embroiled in queer debates, she was forced to admit that such daydreams were bourgeois, the notion of romantic love was inherently heterosexist and the aspiration to family wasn't just politically regressive but also rather embarrassingly old-fashioned. Besides, if gay people aspired to the lives of straight people then, quite logically, gay people would soon be compelled to proscribe themselves.

So, regretfully, Jahanara buried her old love, acquired a girlfriend – or, well, a girl who liked to fuck Jahanara but not *only* Jahanara, abjuring as she did not only marriage and family but also monogamy – and accepted an invitation to Mrinalini and Siddhartha's for dinner.

They hadn't met for almost five years, and Mrinalini was a little jumpy the night before, asking what they should serve, where they should sit, what they should and should not talk about until finally, when Siddhartha emerged from the bathroom and she assailed him with

"You know I think we don't need to have Chhote Lal involved at all. We don't need bhindi and chicken and all those spoons and bowls. Why can't we just have informal dinners ever? Why can't we just order pizza? It doesn't have to be a state banquet every time we call people over, you know" and Siddhartha laughed and said, "Why're you so tense, sweetheart? She's your friend isn't she?"

Mrinalini looked up from the book in her lap and said, "I'm not tense. All I'm saying is, we always have these elaborate, you know, these *meals*, and half the time we're just fussing about food and mixing drinks and, and it just makes me feel *old*. I think it'd be nice if we had a crate of beer and a couple of pizzas and, you know, if we could just talk."

"Okay," he said, "that's not a problem. What beer do you want?"

"I don't know. Any beer. No, that one, Black Label. Jahan says the others are oily."

"Okay. There's this nice one that's come recently, it's South African I think, she might like it, it's called –"

"Maybe we should get whisky also, what do you think? Some nice whisky. What's a nice whisky? Let's get Whitehorse!"

Siddhartha laughed. "Whitehorse is *not* a nice whisky, Leenu. Is that what you guys drank, in Jangpura?"

"Yeah," Mrinalini looked up at him. "It's not good?"

"It's a terrible whisky. You might as well drink a pouch of desi."

"Oh really? We did pass out a lot, it's true."

"Then?" said Siddhartha, getting into bed and taking the book from her hands. "That's what you want to do? Recreate your dissolute youth?"

"You're pretty dissolute yourself," she said, smiling as he leaned forward on his elbows and kissed her mouth. But soon she was saying, "No," and "You lost my page, didn't you?" and "Don't start arguing with her about things, okay?" and Siddhartha rolled away onto his back and said, "Why're you obsessing, yaar? She's not some Queen. And anyway, she didn't even come to our wedding, she obviously doesn't…"

"What?"

"Why're you acting like this is some state visit? And why would I argue?"

"I just mean… you can be snooty sometimes, you know."

"Snooty?"

"Yes. You give the impression that you think anyone who has different ideas is stupid."

"What rubbish. I just don't like people faffing… why, has she become one of those installation artist types? She looked sensible enough in college."

"No. I don't know what she's become. She's doing a PhD in something in JNU…"

"JNU?"

"See? That's what I mean."

'What? What'd I…?"

"The way you said 'JNU', it's just… disapproving."

"Wow. Okay. So I shouldn't ask what she's doing her great PhD in, or where, or in the wrong way…"

"No. Obviously, *ask*. Just don't be snoo– just don't make her uncomfortable, that's all."

"Fine. And? Shall I have my sherwani ironed? Wax my chest?"

"Uff, Siddhartha!"

"Uff, *Mrina*lini. Why're you being so touchy?"

She turned on her side to face him and brought his hand to her lips. He was staring at the ceiling, his wide forehead crinkled in a little-boy's frown.

"I'm not being touchy," she said, wrapping her legs around his and moving her head to his shoulder. "I'm just being touchy-*feely*."

"Hmm…" but she could feel the frown relax and a small shift in his body towards her. She slipped a hand into his pyjamas. "I'm just feeling up my husband. Is that a crime?"

"Hmm…" but now she was certain of a small, unwilling smile, and she felt in herself a reciprocal pleasure, so they made love and for the next half-hour or forty-five minutes there was no need for conversation, and afterwards they both felt better.

Things might have ended there quite happily if Siddhartha hadn't mumbled, "Anyway, I like her. You don't have to worry," turning on to his side and falling fast asleep, unaware of having entirely undone the soporific effects of their lovemaking for his wife, who was now wide awake, troubled by some latent fear she could neither identify nor tame, and spent most of the night in worried dialogue with herself.

They sat in the living room, on furniture that Siddhartha's parents had sent across from their termite-ridden Jor Bagh home – *Get rid of it if you want, they'd assured her, feel free to buy your own preference, but we didn't want you to walk into an empty house!* – shadowed by walls that Mrinalini had had painted a heady shade of purple and which, when they'd had a few drinks,

Jahanara denounced as totally insane, man, what were you thinking? To which Mrinalini replied by laughing unsteadily "Come on! I needed something to distract people from the fucking furniture."

Jahanara glanced at Siddhartha: already they had been speaking as if they had jokes in common, talking politics and food and politely deferring to each others' opinions; now it seemed they were forming a bond against his drunken wife. Not knowing what else to do, Mrinalini asked for another vodka and gulped it down, and just before the pizza arrived, she tumbled gently upon a sofa and fell asleep. Siddhartha, annoyed but gallant, had the table laid and even a fresh salad made to go with their dinner, conducted a perfectly civil conversation for over half an hour, then even offered Jahanara a nightcap. This she refused, as she also refused his offer to drive her home. Maharani Bagh – where she lived, once again, with her parents – was only half a kilometre away: she would walk. She was not afraid of the night, she implied, nor of drunken scenes, nor of marriage vows.

Then, once more, a period of silence engulfed Jahanara and Mrinalini's friendship. This time, a small splash of guilt added to the cocktail of her everlasting hurt, it was Jahanara who proposed a quiet drink somewhere convenient.

Jahanara was always tiny, but she looked even more so that day, sitting across from Mrinalini. Perhaps it had something to do with how she wore her hair, cut almost to the skull and spiky. She still wore men's shirts the way she did in college, but the shirt was fitted now, hanging over straight linen pants that led to a pair of purple shoes. She had developed a new way of talking too – brisk and dry, nothing like the choked avowals of eternal devotion that had marked their brief romance.

They lowered their heads over the menu, reading its every word. It was barely six, and the bar was quiet; a CD of the kind of songs that inspire you to buy jeans at shopping malls played on loop in the background. Only one other table was occupied, by two men, obviously work colleagues, with receding hairlines, incipient paunches and animated conversation.

As her opening gambit, Mrinalini complimented Jahanara's new look and suggested that many of Jahanara's students must nurse secret crushes on her. "Do they?" she asked, smiling broadly. "I bet they do!"

"No doubt. They're teenagers in a convent. They have

crushes on peeling walls. Take your eye off a second and they're marrying posters of the Backstreet Boys."

"Oh come on. I bet you're their favourite – young and hot and gay and everything."

Jahanara laughed half a laugh. "It's not like I have a T-shirt, Mrinalini."

Mrinalini looked into her beer and Jahanara, sensing her embarrassment, said, "No, it's not like they don't have crushes. But it's not much fun when they do, you know. One of them started bringing me roses after every lecture."

Mrinalini looked back up. "I knew it!"

"Seriously, it's a little insulting – all they want is attendance, in the end."

"Even the girl with the roses?"

"*Especially* the girl with the roses. She'd show up once a month with a story so convoluted the rose would have wilted by the time she finished."

"Poor thing!"

"Yeah," said Jahanara, "no need. They're manipulative brats, you don't have to feel sorry for them."

"Well, they're clearly getting no sympathy from *you*," said Mrinalini, raising an eyebrow.

"Will you stop? You're acting like they're underfed

orphans in a sweatshop. Next you'll barge into my classroom and surprise them with some bounty of cardboard boxes for Christmas!"

They looked at each other a moment, then laughed into their beers. Mrinalini said, "Oh Jahan!" and her face lit with a smile, but Jahanara turned down the corners of her mouth, shook her head and muttered "Yeah, whatever…"

The subject changed to people – who had gone where to do what from college, who had stayed behind; who'd dropped into their worlds and who out of them; how many were now married. "Not just married," said Jahanara, "Priya had a baby I heard."

"No, really?"

"Yeah," she nodded and smiled. "I heard from… Facebook. Obviously. Only few months ago."

"Wow. That's really soon though. I didn't think…"

"It's not *that* soon," said Jahanara. She picked up a piece of lukewarm fried fish and dipped it in sauce, pointing it in a fleeting sort of way at Mrinalini before transferring it to her mouth. "You were five already when your mother was your age."

"Yeah," said Mrinalini, frowning, "but that was different."

"Like how?"

"Like just."

"Yeah, but like just how?"

"Oho! Anyway," she raised her eyes to the ceiling, "if my mother had her way, I'd have two squalling monkeys now."

"You mean she's not liberated? Like you?"

If there was an edge to Jahanara's question or tone, Mrinalini ignored it. "Ha-ha-ha-ha," she said, one unflapping 'Ha' at a time. "You're sounding like Brajeshwar."

"Who's Brajeshwar?"

"My tenant," said Mrinalini. "Thinks he's so clever because he's single." And then, "What?" when a self-conscious smile began to spread across Jahanara's face.

"Nothing," she said. "Who says I'm single?"

"You're not? Arre! You never said – you're very secretive, Jahan!"

"You never asked."

"What's to ask? You never said! So tell then? Who is –" she paused a second, "who is she?"

"She's… um…" Jahanara looked down at her glass and then up again. "She's whoever, some…"

"Tell me, tell me Jahan," Mrinalini leaned across the

27

table, a small gurgle of laughter in her voice, "What's she like? Is she a *real* lesbian?"

"What?" Jahanara frowned.

"Is she, you know…"

"Yes, I heard you. A real lesbian? What does that even mean, Mrinalini?"

She said this with such condescension, Mrinalini could only reply, "What's your problem?"

"My problem? Why would you think that was an appropriate question to ask? I mean…"

"I…"

"I mean… what am I? A… a cat? A cat you pat on the head and say, 'Oh good, you found another cat to play with'? I mean, do you have any *notion* of *empathy* at all?"

"I…"

"Man… when're you ever going to start thinking beyond yourself?"

"Man?"

"Yeah. It's the new lesbian lingo. Put it in your notebook."

"Why're you being such a…"

"What?"

"Why're you being so mean?"

"Oh no, so mean! Mrinalini's feelings are hurt. Are you going to cry? Do you want me to take out my lesbian handkerchief? Oh, but wait! Will it fit your big straight nose? God!"

"Jahan…!" Without thinking, Mrinalini touched her nose.

"Fuck this. You know what, Mrinalini? Why don't we save all this meeting and being all friends and shit until you figure out how to care for something in this world that isn't you? Okay?"

"I care for all kinds of thing! I care for *you* obviously, or I'd not be here taking this… this *insult* from you!"

"Insult? Please. You're thrilled to bits, you think I'm having a little jealous breakdown. *God.*"

And, just like that, Jahanara pushed three hundred-rupee notes under the fishfingers and strode off, leaving Mrinalini to remember how she used to call her Loony, and Loony-Toony, and never take her eyes off her even if Mrinalini was only clipping her nails or looking through their tapes for something to play or lying on the mattress and saying she loved Shah Rukh Khan – until she sniffled and had to blow her nose.

2

Scruples and crimes may both be indulged

Some days later, Mrinalini felt in the mood for a change of hair at Khan Market. She was in the drive, unlocking her in-laws' old Maruti 800, when she heard the soft thud of bare feet behind her.

Turning, she saw the small, curly-haired offspring of Chhote Lal and his pretty, newly acquired and much younger wife, Beena. Anjali stopped in her tracks and stared.

"What?" said Mrinalini, flicking her head upwards and smiling. Anjali, accustomed to affection from her parents' employers, grinned back. Anything was possible. Chocolate was possible.

"What?" said Mrinalini again, motioning with her hand for the kid to approach. At this, her grin expanding, Anjali came charging forward. Mrinalini bent low, holding her arms out to greet her, and felt a warm pleasure when Anjali threw herself into her embrace, allowing Mrinalini to raise her high in the air.

"Where are your chappals?"

"Inside," said Anjali, without much interest. "Where are you going?"

"I'm going to the market. Want to come?"

"You're going in the car?"

"Yes. I'm going in the car. Want to come?" Anjali nodded, speechless with glee.

They drove out, Anjali swinging her legs off the back seat and waving at stray dogs perched on the low mounds of sand scattered outside the many old houses in the colony being stretched and drilled into buildings of shining flats. It was only a minute before Mrinalini realized she'd forgotten to tell Beena, lost somewhere inside the house, possibly dusting. They hadn't yet left the colony, and Mrinalini turned the car in a wide loop back to the house. It was barely five minutes since they'd left; Beena was only just walking towards the gate, as yet unaware that her daughter had left the premises, and was as delighted as Anjali herself to see the kid in the back of the blue Maruti, face pressed urgently against its low, half-open window. Only Mrinalini, it seemed, was vaguely relieved to hand the child back to its mother.

Still, from that first unthinking drive flowed other miniscule excursions – a few moments on the roof to admire the view of Sintex tanks, a dash to the local market for cigarettes and bubble-gum – until, one day, Mrinalini and Anjali were gone over two hours and Beena was standing with dry, glazed eyes at the gate when they returned. She snatched Anjali from the auto with such force that the kid's feet banged against the metal floor and Anjali grew teary-eyed with surprise – though she had better sense than to cry. Chhote Lal, standing by their side, had laughed in a nervous, conciliatory way; he had said, "Didi! I told her she was with you. Arre, I was telling her!" – but Beena had turned away so quickly Mrinalini couldn't catch the expression in her eyes, and she sat still, one leg stretched out of the auto, afraid, for a moment, to follow them into her own house.

"It's because I didn't take the car," Mrinalini explained to Siddhartha that evening; they were on their way to a party in Gurgaon. It was a long journey. "She's used to me taking her for rides in the car. That's why she got so hysterical."

"She was hysterical?"

"Yeah. Crying like anything – it's quite silly."

"But how long were you gone?"

"Just… I don't know. Hardly any time. All that happened was, I was walking around with the kid, she likes to see the sights in the lane. I mean she comes running after *me*, it's not like I forced her."

"Yeah…" said Siddhartha, negotiating the overtake of a lurching truck.

"And this empty auto passed and it stopped, you know the way autos do."

"Yeah…"

"And I don't even know what happened. The kid was just jumping about and I thought we could go for a little auto ride, you know? I thought we'll just go to the community centre maybe and have an ice-cream but then I realised I didn't have any money so I told him to take us to India Gate and bring us back. I thought she'd like it – it's good for her to know the city she lives in, isn't it?"

"You had no money?"

"No, obviously. I'd just gone out for a minute."

"And you just got into the auto and drove around? What if he'd stopped somewhere? What if it broke down? What would you have done then?"

"Oho, Siddhartha."

"What 'oho'? It's not safe."

"Of course it's safe. I told him he'll have to bring us back. He was very happy."

"I'm sure he was. But what if his auto broke down? What would you have done then?"

"I don't know! I'd have called you."

"Yeah. Were you even carrying your phone?"

"Yes."

"Don't lie."

"I'm not lying!"

"Oh yeah? Then why didn't Chhote Lal just call you?"

"*I* don't know," Mrinalini rolled her eyes irritably. "I *was* carrying my phone, okay? And all I'm saying is, Beena…"

"Listen, I don't know and I don't really care about Beena. It was a very silly thing to do."

"Okay, okay. I'll never leave home without my wallet. And a first-aid kit. And an inflatable *tube*. Happy?"

"No. Look at this idiot," Siddhartha put his hand on the horn and kept it there, against a speeding motorbike that had cut ahead of him from the wrong side, at a dangerous angle, and was fast disappearing into traffic. "If I was driving like him, he'd be the one dead now, not me."

"Yeah."

"What is he thinking?"

"I don't know."

She waited for Siddhartha's nerves to settle, watching the traffic clear before them as they reached the Delhi-Gurgaon toll road.

"So anyway, that's why," she said.

"Why what?"

"Why I thought we should get her something. Some chocolate or something."

"Chocolate? For Beena?"

"For the kid."

"How'll that help?"

"I don't know," she said, realising the idea made no sense.

"What about Chhote Lal? Is he upset?"

"I don't know…"

"He'd not be hysterical, anyway."

"Why? Because he's a man?"

"Uff. No, yaar. Don't get," Siddhartha drew a breath, "hyper."

"Why then? You're so patriarchal, Siddhartha."

"Because," said Siddhartha, with deliberate calm, "he's been with us forever. He trusts us. And I *know* him, he's a calm fellow."

Mrinalini said nothing. The conversation was making her uncomfortably aware of a lack of legs to stand on, and they drove the rest of the way in silence. Only when they were almost there did Mrinalini say, "It's a difficult drive" – a clear capitulation – and she was grateful for the non-committal "Hmm" he offered in return.

* * *

Things were awkward at home in the days that followed. Beena hovered on the borders of sulky, her eyes to the ground and her mouth downturned – for which Chhote Lal compensated by heaping oil and masala into their dinners, which irritated Siddhartha and threatened to bring out his old complaint about her lack of interest in the kitchen, and precipitate the usual fight.

No doubt, had this occurred, Beena would have been greatly pleased, and perhaps a kind of domestic homeostasis would have brought the house's emotional equilibrium back to normal. In the event, though, what happened was that Siddhartha came home with a swollen cheek, blackening eye and twisted ankle.

"My god," said Mrinalini when he limped through the door, "baby, what happened to you?" She repeated the question, in a high pitch, her eyes wide, nervous yet almost laughing in fear, as she helped him to bed where he lay groaning, as she brought an icepack for his cheek, another for his ankle, as she soaked a towel in warm water and gently cleaned the grit from the scratches on his skin. Then, sitting up on the bed beside him, planting a kiss on his cheek, she said, "Beena's bringing your tea. You'll be fine" – and Siddhartha divulged that he'd got into a fight.

"You don't say?" said Mrinalini, with a smile and a nod, only trying to lighten the mood, but he burst into tears.

This wasn't the first time that Mrinalini had seen Siddhartha cry – it was he who wept on their wedding night, drunken and foolish – but the sight never failed to unnerve her. He was always so brutally frank about his grief.

"Baby?" she whispered, putting a hand on one heaving shoulder, caressing a thigh with the other as he choked on mucus and tears. "Baby," she said, rubbing his back as he hiccupped and breathed and then collapsed once again into an aching, lonely sob. "Baby?" But there was nothing to do but wait. Eventually, his head fell to her lap, she ran her fingers through his hair and he seemed to fall asleep. "Baby?"

What had happened was this: Siddhartha insisted the commute to Gurgaon was no big deal; that he really didn't need a driver. He could drive to Hauz Khas, then take the metro – this gave him time to read the paper, he said, and listen to music. What he could not then admit was how dreary it soon became: the jostling drudgery of it, the standing in line and smelling farts and shuffling always, inwards and outwards. How his temper flared in traffic. On that day, he had emerged at Hauz Khas station to find an SUV parked alongside his Santro, blocking it in. The SUV's driver had ambled off, it seemed; there was no sign of him. Siddhartha sat down behind his wheel and honked, once, twice, then laid his palm on the horn so the street screamed with his protest.

It couldn't have been more than a few minutes, five at most – Siddhartha admitted this – before the SUV's driver returned. Perhaps he had merely hopped out for a pee. But something about his lazy, unapologetic gait so incensed Siddhartha that he leaped out of his car and began to yell, accusing the driver of incompetence and idiocy bordering on the criminal. The driver responded in kind, and Siddhartha raised a hand, adding insolence to his list of the man's shortcomings and telling him to mind his tongue. Unmindful, the driver punched him in the face. Siddhartha fell to the ground and would, no doubt, have suffered broken bones or worse if a crowd hadn't gathered and cajoled the SUV's driver away.

Lifting himself up, enraged and screaming, Siddhartha twisted his own ankle. The journey home was agony.

The next day, Siddhartha called in sick. The day after, too. A week passed and his swellings subsided and on Sunday it seemed like he was well enough to return to work, but then he said, "You know what?"

"Tell?" Mrinalini spoke with a conscious kindness, as she had spoken every day since his collapse. She did not want to witness another test of his fragility.

"I think I'm going to quit."

"Quit what?"

"Quit banking! What d'you think?"

She smiled, surprised at how the idea made her happy.

"Really? Your job?"

"Yeah!" He looked younger as he said it.

"But how come?"

"Why, you thought only you can live the bohemian life?"

He said it with great affection, though, not in the irritable tone he might have used before, so she hugged him and she said, "Then what. I thought you'll never join me!"

Siddhartha hugged her back and kissed her forehead and brought out his American accent and said, "Carpe the diem, baby!" and he laughed and she laughed too and she said, "Okay."

"Okay then," he replied.

Siddhartha didn't let the momentum slide. He quit on Monday, without even telling his parents; by the end of the week he was a man free to linger over a second cup of bed-tea and remain unshaven all day.

Mrinalini, who hadn't been sure how she'd react to having a husband at home, found that she liked it. She liked how his body lingered next to hers in the morning, how he remained in bed, keeping it warm for her to slide back in with the newspaper. They both rediscovered how much they enjoyed making love in the afternoon, when the sounds of the neighbourhood fell to their lowest murmur, the houses empty of bread-earners, the servants relieved of duty until tea-time, even the ubiquitous drone of construction somewhere along the lane muffled and apologetic.

Siddhartha's was a calm, cheerful presence in these first few weeks of holiday. He brought her mid-morning cups of coffee with a kiss; he pottered in the kitchen instructing Chhote Lal in the fine art of the risotto, the pakchoi, the khausuey; he sat on the verandah in a happy pile of newspapers and magazines, available, should she want him, to call the broadband people to fix the internet or the electrician to fix the AC or... well, be useful, which is what he enjoyed being.

It was on one such day, in fact, as Siddhartha lay on the freshly-made bed, reading a frayed biography of some financial genius and Mrinalini walked out from the bathroom, unwrapped the towel from her head and filled the air with the fruity scent of her shampoo, that Mrinalini experienced a sudden lifting of gravity that dropped her many feet further in love.

She examined the feeling, leaving it alone to settle, prodding it this way and that to see if it might

41

dissipate, testing it against Siddhartha's growing propensity to snore, or to waltz blindly into her study with a taste of sauce for her to pass in the middle of a sentence.

Eventually, she told him.

"Is that so?" said Siddhartha. His pleasure was shy: a slow smile suffused his features.

"Look at you!" said Mrinalini, pleased. "I think you're blushing!"

"No!"

But he was. A little. They were sitting side-by-side on a sofa in the drawing room, sipping wine before dinner. Mrinalini had sacrificed her pre-dinner vodka and writing hour to inaugurate a new ritual: Siddhartha thought it would be fun to "eat out at home" once a week; tonight, there was grilled fish and roast potatoes and, just to spice things up, a Thai green mango salad. Dessert was secret.

"You are," said Mrinalini with a grin, "blushing like a girl."

"Well," said Siddhartha, reversing the curve of his lips, trying to be cool, "just as well, then, that I don't have to worry…"

"Worry about what?"

"I mean I have all this extra time for all this extra love. Otherwise, with my busy and very important life, you'd probably feel quite neglected."

"So funny," she said, smacking his shoulder.

"Women would be chasing me in the boardroom and you'd be crying on the sofa, singing sad songs…"

"Shuttup Sid – I'm changing my mind!"

"No, no!" He leaned over and kissed her mouth. "Never!" He smiled into her eyes. "You know, I was *actually* thinking, I've *been* thinking," his eyes were open and frank. She raised an eyebrow. "I mean, I guess if I don't have a job for a while, maybe I could do something – like study, maybe…"

"Is that what you want to do?"

"I was thinking."

"It's a great idea. Yes. Oh –"

"You think so?" That shy smile again.

"Oh, yes. Definitely. Going to college again, that's a fantastic idea."

"Well, I was only thinking," he said, modestly. "But if I do…"

"You absolutely should!"

"You think so? I'm really happy, because I was worried…"

"Why?"

"I mean, it might mean…" he laughed, "well, it *will* mean a little less, you know…"

"What?"

"Well… money, I guess."

"Money! How you worry about money all the time, Sid! It's just paper…"

"Yeah." His laughter was relieved, and they both raised their glasses and swallowed their wine in a toast, and Siddhartha left to retrieve the bottle from the fridge.

With him gone, running her hands along an ornately carved arm of teak, Mrinalini felt strangely abandoned. She shook her head to steady herself but the feeling persisted. How did it matter, she shrugged, a little less money? With all this time and freedom at their disposal, how would it hurt to splurge a little less on whatever citronella-scented establishment serving dainty helpings of water-chestnuts by another name surfaced in South Delhi next? But by the time Siddhartha returned, she wasn't sure whether to curse or console him – him and all his eating-out-at-home business. Well now she knew, didn't she: they couldn't afford the real thing.

Siddhartha poured carefully, letting the wine out in a niggling trickle, until she'd worked herself to such impatience that she took the glass from him with a jerk that sent the liquid sloshing from side to side like a sea in storm, and a few drops spilled over the rim. Mrinalini took a long swallow, looked up at her husband and smiled, hoping the panic didn't show in her eyes.

Siddhartha applied for a two-year advanced programme at the Indian Institute of Finance and a one-year MPhil at the Delhi School of Economics, and didn't make it to either. You couldn't blame him; the applicant-to-seat ratio was ridiculously daunting and it would have been something of a minor miracle if he had.

This initial failure didn't seem to make him particularly unhappy, though, and Siddhartha began to talk tentatively of joining cooking classes – maybe even a reputable diploma course abroad? – but at this his father drew the line and quickly had him appointed Young Professional in the service of Member (Development Policy, Perspective Planning & International Economics) at the Planning Commission. He was sanctioned a small office with an asthmatic old air-conditioner, located between a peon-infested corridor and a concrete wall, and his monthly take-home was about a fifth of what he'd made at the bank.

Even so, Mrinalini was impressed. Her husband was In Government, and the GoI had long been, to both their families, an avuncular entity, generous in the disbursement of allowances and pensions, and skilled in deploying its red tape in such a way that you felt you belonged and deserved just a little bit more than everybody on the other side.

"In the end," she said to Siddhartha, when he asked once more if she would cope with their straitened means, "you'll be at the heart of it, seeing how all these decisions are made and everything! It's totally worth it."

Plus, she couldn't help the occasional, fleeting daydream of how, when he eventually returned to the market, this brisk constitutional through the corridors of power would catapult his worth.

Meanwhile, Mrinalini had the house to herself once again, a fact she greeted with both pleasure and trepidation. On the one hand, she was free to laze through a day without Siddhartha having to know about it. On the other hand, there was Beena.

When Siddhartha was around, the servants seemed to become half-visible. With him gone, Mrinalini returned to tiptoeing around Beena, dashing to the safety of her study, eating her lunch in hurried bites. She avoided Anjali too, declaring sternly that she was busy whenever the child made an appearance – which wasn't, she had to admit, as often as before. Beena had taken to leaving her in their quarter, claiming she was asleep or should be.

A week passed and Mrinalini grew impatient, with herself and the maid. This was her house, after all, she needn't hide in it, cooped up in the study; she could watch a movie with equal legitimacy. It was the kind of thing she had done quite often in the past, bought a film before lunch to watch it on Siddhartha's beloved 42-inch screen.

(Then, she would usually snap the DVD back into its case, slip the case into its plastic cover, and leave it on the table as if intending it for the evening's entertainment. On those few occasions that she admitted to having already seen the film, he was grievously hurt and she felt cruel for days afterwards.)

In any case, she did not set out to buy a film that day; she went to get a decent cup of coffee, to sit in Barista and have an affogato. Mrinalini loved affogatos: she loved the ice-cream melting in the bitter coffee, she loved the tiny, graceful finitude of it all. A scoop, a sip and it is done.

Had the waiter not indicated that she should order something to go with her drink, Mrinalini might have left satisfied. Had he not been rather more enthused than called for, asking her to choose from the vast variety on their refurbished menu, smiling at her in his young way, and making her suddenly and terribly self-conscious, wondering whether 200 rupees wasn't too much for a brownie – she might not have left feeling just that crucial bit less than satiated, twitchingly underspent.

So, Mrinalini wandered into the local DVD shop. Forty minutes of browsing through stacks of movies that neither compelled her interest nor fizzled it out produced a headache, but it was too late to leave without actually buying something. She ran her fingers over stacks of DVD spines hoping for a spark to blaze and stopped at *Pyaasa*.

Only the other day, at that Gurgaon party in fact, where she'd been introduced to the token intellectual type among the financiers on the basis of her novel-writing ambitions, Mrinalini had been acutely embarrassed at having unthinkingly admitted she'd never seen it. "Haven't seen *Pyaasa*?" he had cried, waggling his token intellectual beard in indignation. "But you want to be a writer! Tell me you've heard the songs, at least?"

At this, Mrinalini had nodded impatiently. "Yes, yes," she had said, though at that moment she had no idea what the songs might be.

"*Yeh duniya agar mil bhi jaaye…*" he'd begun to sing, with exaggerated and tuneless emotion.

"Yes, yes." She had, of course, heard the dolorous melody, "Of course I've seen it, as a kid."

"But you have to see it now! Just drop everything and get the video. Get everything Guru Dutt ever made!"

So there it was – *but you want to be a writer*, indeed! – and having spotted it, she bought the damn thing. Back home, shortly after noon, Mrinalini popped the film in the player and installed herself before the screen, half-aware of the jangle of Beena's bangles as she went about the house with her duster, and the sound of lunch being prepared in the kitchen. She was quite sure it wasn't even *that* great. Only a few minutes passed before Mrinalini proved herself right. She was entirely underwhelmed. For a homeless poet wandering the streets, Guru Dutt looked remarkably well fed. She wondered if her phone was ringing; she had left it in the other room.

Still, the songs of *Pyaasa* she *had* heard before, and while her mind wandered through the plot, each melody brought back a comfortable feeling of childhood. She found herself humming along, not even looking straight at the screen, and suddenly she was back in their old cantonment house in Ranikhet, its floors thickly carpeted and the fire blazing. There was the clink of ice-cubes in her father's glass, there was the soft click-clack of her mother's knitting, there was a distant howl that might be the wind sweeping over mountains or a leopard's complaint against the world. She understood what it meant for something to touch a chord, for it seemed as if her heart expanded with every note, growing youthful and more loving and able, somehow, to understand every particle of her existence. Now, she felt, now was the time to write it all down.

She left the DVD running and walked out to fetch her laptop, and outside the door she found Beena in tears. The sight irritated Mrinalini. Moments of inspiration were few and she hated wasting them. She wished there was some way she could pretend she hadn't seen the red eyes that now looked away from her, following the sweep of a broom. With reluctance, then, and some distaste, Mrinalini said, "What happened Beena? Are you crying?"

"No, no, didi," said Beena, wiping at her cheeks with her free hand.

"What's the matter?"

"Nothing didi, nothing."

At this, she could have resumed her course laptop-wards, quite free of guilt – if Beena didn't want to tell her, then that was Beena's business. But now, having her concern brushed away, Mrinalini felt even more irritated than she had at having to express any in the first place. What did it mean, this 'nothing-nothing'? That there was no point telling Mrinalini her troubles? That she would have preferred a higher authority – Siddhartha perhaps, or his mother – to hear her case? So, Mrinalini persevered. "Is Anjali all right?"

"Yes, didi, she's fine. She's fine."

"Is everything okay at home?"

"Yes, didi. Everyone is fine at home."

Excluding some dire sorrow purely of the soul, this left only the husband. "And Chhote Lal?" said Mrinalini, unconsciously lowering her voice and glancing towards the kitchen.

"He's fine. How else will he be, didi?"

"What do you mean?"

"What can I say, didi?" Beena had slipped past her into the bedroom and Mrinalini half-closed the door. "He says I don't take care of Anjali."

"Don't take care of Anjali?"

"He says I don't take care of her. Don't feed her, don't teach her. He says I don't know how to be a mother."

"Oh," said Mrinalini, taken aback. She hadn't ever investigated Beena's maternal skills, but she'd heard her calling Anjali for meals, and seen her washing Anjali under the tap. How much more could you want her to love the kid?

"But why?" she asked. Beena had returned her mournful gaze to the floor.

"Who knows? This is what he says."

"But why?" she asked again. "Has something happened? Did you have a fight?"

"What is the use of fighting, didi? But every day there is a fight."

"*Yes*," said Mrinalini, a little irritation seeping into her tone at this speaking in riddles, "but what about?"

Embarrassment flickered on Beena's face; then she seemed to make a decision. "He drinks," she said, looking up at Mrinalini.

Mrinalini opened her mouth to reply and felt a slight heat in her cheeks. She looked away. *Drinks*, indeed. If Mrinalini liked a glass or two of vodka every evening, what business was that of Beena's? Chhote Lal was the *cook*, for god's sake.

"What do you mean? He's worked here for years. I hope he's not drinking on duty?"

"I don't know," said Beena, sullen now and staring at the ground.

Mrinalini sighed and wondered whether to call Siddhartha immediately or to wait till lunch.

It was comforting, as always, that when Siddhartha came home and found Mrinalini fiddling with Facebook in bed, he said, "It's okay. It's all taken care of."

"Is it?" Mrinalini sat up with unusual alacrity. "Because I found out a whole lot more. You want to know? It's *quite* the scandal."

"It is? Scandal?" Siddhartha sat down beside her

and began taking off his shoes. "So what's the scandal, then?" he folded his legs on the bed and smiled.

"Oh god. Where to begin?"

"Begin, begin!"

"Well, first of all," said Mrinalini, "your Chhote Lal's an alcoholic… though I don't know how he's been all this time without anyone noticing – according to Beena he's drunk breakfast onwards every day. But that you know…"

"That you told me…"

"That I told you. And when I told you I'd sent her off because her crying was giving me a headache then I felt bad and I called her again after lunch. And now she tells me: firstly he's spending all their money on booze, then he's gone all patriarchal on her and is accusing her," she paused, "of *having affairs*."

"Yeah," said Siddhartha, smiling still but a little sheepish, "I know."

"You know! What do you know? No, Sid, he found the upstairs fellow, Braj's guy, that what's-his-name, he found him in their room, he was sitting on the bed it seems, and now he says she's having an affair with him!" She looked at him. "You know this?"

"No, no… this I don't know. But I heard…"

"Heard? How? Chhote Lal's been bitching to you?"

"No, yaar," said Siddhartha in that way he had, being impatient to mask some embarrassment or irritation. "I spoke to Mama."

Given how she had stipulated no role in domestic affairs when they were married – "Listen, Sid, don't ask me to spend my life cooking bhindi and worrying about how many litres of milk the servants are drinking, okay? *Promise* me" – Mrinalini could hardly blame her mother-in-law for being more fully abreast of these matters than she was, nor react to Siddhartha's revelation with more than a small "Oh."

"Chhote Lal told her, it seems."

"Sure," said Mrinalini, trying to mask her deflation, though evidently with little success, since Siddhartha leaned forward and began massaging her feet.

"Because, you know, he's been with us for years. She calls him, what to do?"

"Of course, yes," said Mrinalini, drawing her feet away ungraciously. Siddhartha's mother did, indeed, call Chhote Lal – 'once in a while' was the family phrase for it, but Mrinalini suspected 'every other minute' would be a closer description, if not of the truth then certainly of the spirit of her enquiry.

"So then," she said, relinquishing all hold on the matter, "what's the goss?"

Siddhartha drew his hands back into his lap and faced her cross-legged, his expression still conciliatory and benign. "So the thing is this," he said.

"Yeah?"

He tried again. "Well she is…" again he stopped.

"What?"

"So!" he said and laughed as if that was some kind of joke. Mrinalini raised an eyebrow. "Okay, so, Mama says we could consider letting her go back…"

Siddhartha always spoke of his mother as "Mama", elevating the endearment to a title. Mrinalini preferred "my mother"; amongst people she considered strangers she might contract the description to "my mum", so it was no surprise that she referred to Siddhartha's mother as "my mother-in-law" or, to him, "your mother". She knew he'd like her to say "Mama" too, sinking into the warmth of the word, but she couldn't, and wouldn't, even if it made her seem distant or, as now – "I don't understand, your mother said *what*?" – confrontational.

"Look, it's nothing. She just suggested maybe we should send her back to the village if her being here is going to cause, you know, problems."

"Problems? Like what problems? He's the one drinking, remember?"

"Well, look, I don't know. Have you ever seen him drunk? I mean, if it's just a couple of pegs at night or something…"

"Yes, but why would she be so upset then? He's obviously spending all their money on booze."

"I don't know. He keeps buying that kid all those clothes and toys. He obviously loves her."

"Yes, but…"

"And look, this girl, she's much younger than him, isn't she? I mean, who knows?"

"Who knows what?"

"Just, I mean. Who knows what their marriage is like?"

"Fine," said Mrinalini, with a surge of anger, "and what about the kid then? What's going to happen to *her* in that village then?"

"Haan… Well, it's not a final decision, is it? It's us, we'll decide."

"Right. So what else did she say?"

"Who?"

"Your mother!"

"Nothing. Don't get hyper, yaar. But it's true, we've

57

had him forever. Chhote Lal's been around since Gautam was born – I mean, we trust him."

"So you think she's lying? Beena?"

"Look, don't ask me. I don't know."

"You just said you trust *him*…"

"Yes well," he paused and took a breath. "I said we *have* to trust him, he's been around so long. And she, well, she's just come, hasn't she?"

"Beena you mean? She has a name."

"Yeah, fine. Her."

"And I'm the only one who's spoken to her, not you or your mother, by the way."

"There's no need to blame Mama for this."

"I'm not blaming anyone." She resisted the impulse to roll her eyes, it would only infuriate him, and his fury on his mother's behalf was always unpleasant. "I just don't think we should be so quick to blame Beena, actually."

"Sure, okay. Maybe it'll just blow over. People have fights."

"Yeah, but I think you should talk to Chhote Lal anyway; tell him to calm down."

Reluctantly, Siddhartha agreed; and he returned from the servant's quarter to report that things were bad and liable to get worse. "He's insisting Brajeshwar's fellow and this girl are having an affair – it's got into his head like a worm. I just hope they don't try killing each other."

"Did you ask about the drinking?"

"You know, I really don't think that's such a big deal. He admits he likes a drink, but it's hardly a problem. He says he knows what his responsibilities are. He says he could hardly have worked for so many years, and it's true… you don't have to roll your eyes."

"Fine. He's loyal, he's a saint. So now what to do?"

"Arre yaar. How do I know? We can wait and watch, see who beats the other's brains out first."

"Hmm."

"Or somebody has to leave. I mean… you agree, right? Just one of them has to go and we'll be fine."

"Hmm."

"So I don't know. You want to ask Brajeshwar to sack his fellow?"

"Uff…"

"Well that's right. So it's either Chhote Lal or…"

"Hmm."

"Anyway," he said, "there it is."

Some ten days passed in relatively peaceful

indecision. Beena's eyes were sometimes red and Chhote Lal's voice was gruff, but the housework got done and no particularly alarming sounds emanated from their quarter at night.

Then, one day, they woke to find Chhote Lal walking with a slight limp. When Siddhartha asked what happened, the older man laughed and replied, "Arre, nothing baba, nothing! Just fell a little."

"You should be careful then. Isn't that the leg you broke?"

"Yes baba, but what to do?"

"What to do? Be careful, that's what," said Siddhartha and Mrinalini echoed the sentiment from over her lemon water. Chhote Lal's broken leg had had them ordering out for months, sent Siddhartha's temper soaring, and come close to critically endangering their marriage.

They had only just returned their eyes to their newspapers when the bell rang and their upstairs tenant rushed into the bedroom. "You guys are damn calm, I must say!"

"What?" Siddhartha sat up and slipped his feet into slippers; Mrinalini pulled her sheet an inch higher towards her neck.

"You don't know? Harish is in hospital, soaking his sheets in blood!"

"Harish?"

"My fellow!"

"What?"

"That's what I'm saying. Stab wound. According to him, inflicted by your fellow, so you'd better wake up. I thought the police would be here by now."

On cue, Beena burst wailing into the room. "Bhaiyya!" she cried, "Police!"

Holding up a hand to silence her, Siddhartha turned to Brajeshwar, "What the hell is going on?"

"God fucking knows, man. I got a call at some five this morning, there's a woman having hysterics on the other end. Turns out Harish is in hospital and bleeding and the doctors want money and they want to call the police and all kinds of surreal shit is going on. So I went, of course, and there he is, half alive and he says your guy stabbed him."

"Chhote Lal?"

"Yeah."

The bell rang again. "Police!" cried Beena and Anjali ran to hide behind her legs. Siddhartha strode to the kitchen and the rest of them followed. The bell rang again; in the kitchen it was loudest and Mrinalini felt goosebumps rise on her arms. Chhote Lal, too, seemed to jump a little and then lunged dramatically at Siddhartha's feet, his frame extending almost the entire length of the narrow, rectangular room.

"Get up!" said Siddhartha, "get up! There's no time for this. What have you been doing?"

"Forgive me, baba! Forgive me!" and the bell rang one-two-three, its shrill call ricocheting from wall to wall.

"Open the door, Beena!" Siddhartha was almost shouting.

"I'll go," Mrinalini muttered and turned to follow Beena. When the door opened to reveal two tall, unsmiling, khaki-clad policemen, guns hanging loosely at their hips, Anjali, who'd been clutching her mother's legs, burst into tears.

"Madam," said one of the men above the uproar, but Anjali would have none of it. She screamed with greater vigour. Both the policemen and Mrinalini teetered a step backwards, and Mrinalini held up a finger to indicate that they wait a minute. She turned to Beena and said, "Take her inside?" but Beena, perhaps suspecting that only this sobbing gale kept the police at bay, refused to budge.

Not knowing what to do, Mrinalini stepped out into the driveway and closed the door behind her. "Madam," said the first policeman again, looking relieved, "we are seeking one Chhote Lal. He works for you. Is he inside?"

"Yes, but what has he done?"

"Madam, we don't know and we can't say. But he is accused of attacking and stabbing your other servant —"

"Upstairs."

"Right. Your upstairs servant is admitted in hospital, emergency, wounded. He is," he turned to his colleague who muttered "Harish." "Right. Harish accuses your Chhote Lal of attacking him. We have only come to question him and to establish the truth. Nothing more or less than that."

"But he's been with us forever," she said, producing her only argument. "We trust him."

"Madam," said the policeman, inflating his chest, "Let me tell you from our experience that all criminals are greatly trustworthy. You can trust them to rob their mothers, kill their fathers and rape their daughters. That," he concluded with a dry chuckle, "is a fact. Come. Let us go inside."

Mrinalini, uncomfortably aware of the flimsiness of her nightie as the morning air filtered through to her skin, crossed her arms across her breasts and was fighting the urge to run indoors and turn the lock, when Siddhartha stepped out. "Yes," he said, in his most authoritative tone, "tell me what's going on." As the policeman began to speak, Siddhartha turned to Mrinalini, "Why don't you go inside?" he said. "The kid and mother are both…"

"Okay," she said, and fled.

* * *

The house was emptied of men: Siddhartha, Brajeshwar and Chhote Lal had all three proceeded with the policemen to the local station. This left Beena free to cry while her daughter clung to her lap and Mrinalini stood at a dainty distance from the stove, stirring grains of black tea into a pot of boiling, sugary milk. She poured a large mug for Beena and handed it to her. "Here, drink this. Have you even eaten any breakfast? Do you want some toast?" Beena shook her head, desolate, and seemed inclined to reject even the tea, so Mrinalini said, "Okay, but drink the tea. It'll help. You need to be strong now."

Mrinalini made toast anyway, one for herself, another for Anjali, and chewed standing up. Beena's tears slowed to a trickle. They waited. When Siddhartha called, eventually, it was to say they'd take a while. He wouldn't elaborate, but he said not to worry. Mrinalini relayed the message to Beena, who was staring at the floor and barely nodded in acknowledgement. Anjali had fallen asleep, and Mrinalini suggested that Beena should try and take her mind off things by doing some dusting. She could put Anjali into their bed.

Beena had gathered her duster and was drifting dolefully about the house, Mrinalini had resumed the reading of her newspaper, and just the pretence of normalcy was beginning to take soothing effect, when the small body on the bed stirred and let out a mumbled cry.

"Oh!" Mrinalini walked to the bed and sat on its edge, "What happened?"

Another small cry.

"What happened darling?"

The mouth opened to bawl and Mrinalini covered it quickly with her hand. "Shh! What's there to cry about? Mummy's coming, everything's fine. Shh!"

Taken aback by this sudden intimacy, Anjali hiccupped.

"What happened?" Mrinalini withdrew her hand and wiped a little spittle on the bedcover. "Did you have a bad dream?"

But Anjali, ungagged, seemed unwilling to enter rational discourse. With a great gasping breath, she let forth an animal howl. Mrinalini, startled to her feet, was hovering by the bed, holding her palms out in a calming manner, attempting to pat the kid's head when Beena hurried into the room.

"What happened, Anju, what happened?"

Stepping away awkwardly, Mrinalini gestured for Beena to sit.

"Anju, what happened?"

"Crocodile," Anjali whispered.

"What, what?"

"Crocodile!" she said again, louder.

"It was just a bad dream, Anju!"

"The crocodile came in our room."

"Arre! Then what happened?"

"Crocodile came in our room to eat the baby, but all the mummies came and hit him and he ran away!"

"Well that's good! Then the baby was saved?"

"Haan! But then the baby crocodile remained behind, nobody sawed him."

"Oh my god! Even the mummies didn't saw him?"

"They *could*n't saw him, he was so small. How could they catch him?"

"But then?"

"Then… the crocodile came back."

"The same crocodile?"

"Haan! Crocodile came back and ate up the baby. And he ate up you also and he ate up Papa also and he ate up Nani also and he ate up Nana also."

There was a pause. Beena wiped the tears off her daughter's cheeks.

"And it ate up –"

"Didn't it get a tummy ache?" asked Mrinalini.

"It ate up the baby also and the baby's Mummy and the baby's Papa and the baby's –"

"And his tummy didn't start hurting? From eating too much?"

"No." Anjali looked at Mrinalini with some pity. "His tummy was fine. Duck's tummy started hurting."

"Duck?"

"Haan! Duck came and ate up the crocodile!"

"Really?"

"Ya!"

"And what were you doing in all this? Did you help the duck?"

"I was," she said, "I was helping the duck. I was telling Nana crocodile likes babies."

"You told him?"

"I told him, but Nana washes me inside the river. I told him the crocodile will come."

"In your dream, you told him?"

"In the village!"

"Oh! Your nana takes you for your bath in the river?"

"Haan! I don't like it."

"But darling, if your nana is there, no crocodile will come, I'm sure."

"Crocodile likes babies."

"But you're not a baby are you? Anjali's not a baby is she? The crocodile will probably be more scared of you!" She emphasised her point by tapping the tip of Anjali's nose with a finger, and glanced at Beena. For the first time in months, the two women smiled at each other. Then, Beena stood up and scooped Anjali to the ground. "Come," she said, "want to go to the bathroom, now?"

* * *

The rest of the day passed in a state of diffused panic strangely akin to boredom. Siddhartha called a few times, but wouldn't say much; Beena threw up with worry. Siddhartha's mother called and spoke regretfully of what happens when servants marry and bring their wives to the city. "This is what happens," she said.

It was dark when the bell rang. Mrinalini was sitting with her legs splayed on the coffee table, Anjali was perched on an adjacent chair, Beena stood behind them; all three faced the TV, glowing like a primordial fire against the lonesome howl of winter.

Beena had reached the door before Mrinalini could stand up. She heard Siddhartha's voice and followed. "Hey," he said, and behind him said Brajeshwar, "God I need a drink!" A sheepish-looking Chhote Lal limped in last, and Siddhartha turned to ask for ice and soda.

"Chhote Lal ji," said Mrinalini, "everything okay?" Chhote Lal looked away without reply.

"Yeah, yeah," said Siddhartha impatiently, and led them into the living room, where he found the whiskey and was soon busy pouring.

"Then?" It was a relief to have sound and light in the house, the growl of the air-conditioner, Brajeshwar's shoes against the floor and in the background a soft clatter in the kitchen.

"Then what? Where to begin?" Siddhartha held all three glasses in two hands and distributed them with a poise that seemed to underline his ability to handle everything.

"Sex and murder, Mrin Singh, sex and murder most foul it was," Brajeshwar took a gulp of his drink and laughed, "oh and I forget: Cheers!"

They raised their glasses.

"Cheers," said Mrinalini, doubtfully. Both the exclamation and nicknaming seemed unduly precipitate. "So it's really all sorted?"

"I hope –"

"For the moment, at least, your loyal retainer's safe; you might want to have him patted down for sharp instruments at nightfall, though."

"Tell, no?" She turned to Siddhartha. "What happened?"

"Arre, what will happen," said Brajeshwar, bringing out his cigarettes and offering them around. Gratefully, Mrinalini reached for the packet. "How long was it, Sid? Ten hours, rescuing our criminal mastermind."

"How's Harish?"

"Never better. Twenty thousand richer."

"Siddhartha?"

He shrugged.

"But… so I mean, what? This fellow actually stabbed him?"

"So that's not *his* story," said Brajeshwar, emptying his glass. Siddhartha rose to get a refill. "His story, if you can believe it, is… well."

"Yes? What?"

"Okay, so…. He admits he got drunk, right Sid?"

"Yeah." There was between them the ease of having together participated in a small but memorable bit of history, as if they had returned from watching a tense cricket match.

"That he'll admit, and he had a fight with your woman. You know how it is, he says. Told her she was a lying-cheating whore, that kind of thing, but in an amiable sort of way, he insists. Hardly worth getting upset about. *Then* he thought, why confine myself to the wife, won't it be a good idea to go and find the other accused? Enter poor Harish, god-fearing, happily-married with two kids, but nonetheless. So he went stumbling off into these mohallas in the back where Harish lives…"

"And he took a knife?"

"Now that's the thing. It seems all your man wanted to do was have a little chat. At 2.00 am. He only wanted to establish the fact that listen, if you're fucking my wife don't think I don't know about it, sim –"

"Well, not that simple," Siddhartha waved at Mrinalini's smoke rising towards him. "He does say he took the knife because it was late. For his own safety."

"Okay. Then?"

"Well, now, neither of them is telling us what they talked about, you see," Siddhartha spoke as if, any minute now, he would turn to a screen behind him and point a small laser at a graph. "Chhote Lal admits it got heated, but he insists his intention wasn't to get physically violent in any way. He broke his leg, remember? He wouldn't want to take any chances. So the story is, and this is the story we're all sticking to," he glanced at Brajeshwar, "that there was a brief tussle and Chhote Lal slipped."

"Slipped?"

"Slipped and slippery-slipped a knife in poor Harish's arm. Just below the shoulder, but it's not a deep wound. I mean, they didn't even take him to the hospital till some three hours later."

"And that's what Harish says?"

"Well that's what he says *now*, isn't it? That's what took us all this time, reminding him what actually happened."

"Look," said Siddhartha, putting up a hand, but Brajeshwar wasn't fighting.

"No, no, I agree this is better for everyone. Harish took forever to catch on. Probably the painkillers."

"And the police?"

"Police didn't care, yaar. They were being damn sweet. Sid's dad made a phone call and then we got our tea."

She looked at Siddhartha who grimaced.

"Your mother called," she said, remembering.

"Oh. Yeah."

"You must have spoken…"

"Yeah, she's very worried. And you know how fond…" Siddhartha turned to Brajeshwar, "Mama's very fond of Chhote Lal. He's been around forever."

"Sure."

There was a brief silence.

"So…" said Mrinalini, as Brajeshwar exclaimed,

"Forbidden love! Right here in our midst! D'you think it's true? Sid's being too superior, but you have to say Mrin. What d'you think?"

She laughed. "You mean Sid won't play with you?"

"Exactly right. Such a solid fellow, Harish, and damn good cook also. No romantic hero, you know. No Aurangzeb he."

"Aurangzeb?"

"Ha!" said Siddhartha. He'd obviously heard the story.

"What?" said Mrinalini, frowning.

"Arre!" Brajeshwar leaned back in his armchair, stretching his long legs before him, and held his empty glass up for Siddhartha, about to begin, but just then Beena walked in with a bowl of roasted peanuts and chopped onions, another of steaming pakoras nestled around a bowl of red sauce.

"What's all this?" asked Siddhartha.

"Snacks," she said to the table on which she placed the bowls. They were silent as she arranged the small plates and napkins, but she hadn't quite left, was just walking out of the room when Brajeshwar laughed. The air tingled with embarrassment.

"What's so funny?" asked Mrinalini.

"Nothing, nothing," but he wouldn't stop laughing.

"What?" she said again, raising her eyes to Siddhartha who loomed above them with their refills,

"What, what?" But Siddhartha only smiled, if a little tightly.

"What?"

"You've heard of blood money, right?" said Brajeshwar, laughing through a gulp, "So meet blood pakoras," he took one and dipped it in the sauce and transferred it to his mouth. In the chewing, at least, there was some silence.

"He's feeling guilty, I think," said Siddhartha, almost apologetic.

"You think!" Brajeshwar swallowed. "He'll be feeding you pakoras of his heart if you let him."

When Brajeshwar had left, greatly cheerful and a little drunk, and Beena had taken Anjali off to the quarter, subdued and red-eyed, and Chhote Lal had bid them a most fawning goodnight and headed off towards his own quarter of rum, and Mrinalini and Siddhartha were free to have a nightcap or brush their teeth and climb into bed, they walked slowly and separately, switching off lights and tugging at curtains along the way, to the bedroom, where Siddhartha stretched himself on the bed and exhaled a long, sighing "Aah!"

"Long day," Mrinalini caressed his feet

sympathetically on her way to the bathroom. When she emerged, bathed and changed and smelling of talc, his eyes were closed and she was wondering whether to wake him when he said, "How're you?"

"Okay," she replied, touched and relieved. "We were all worried."

"Yeah. Sorry, sweetheart. It took so long."

"No, I know. Of course. Beena was most worried, I guess. She vomited."

"Oh yeah?" he opened his eyes and looked at her, a long, tired look. Unthinkingly, she pressed the tip of his nose with her finger. He shook her hand away, smiling, and sat up, lingering on the edge of the bed a while, as if to gather his forces. For a moment, she had a vision of him as an old man.

To his back she posed the question in her head. "So?"

"So… what?"

"So what's the decision? Does she go?"

"I…" Siddhartha, too, seemed to prefer conducting the conversation without eye contact. "That seems like the most sensible thing to do, doesn't it?"

"And the kid?"

"And… yeah."

He rose and walked into the bathroom and closed the door. When he returned, Mrinalini had got into bed and was pretending to be asleep. He wrapped an arm around her, letting his hand rest just below her breasts the way he liked it to.

They had lain like this a while when Mrinalini made up her mind. "Sid?" she said, "are you awake?"

"Hmm…" he didn't sound awake.

"Listen, Sid?"

"*Hmm!*"

"I want to keep them."

"Hmm…"

"The kid, and Beena. Let's keep them? I'll take care of her, I'll… I'll…"

"Hmm?"

"I'll teach her English. She's *scared* of crocodiles in her village. Sid?" she turned to face him, talking into his ear. "Tell your mother? *I'll* handle it."

"Hmm…"

"Okay?"

"Oh Leenu…"

"Sid!"

"Fine… fine. If you care so much. Sleep now?"

"Fine."

"Hmm..."

In the dark silence, Mrinalini smiled. *Now* let Jahanara say she didn't care about anything except herself. Let her.

3

It's caring that has you decidedly vexed

Mrinalini's first act of selfless giving was to have Anjali admitted into a local preschool called Sing-a-Song. At first, Mrinalini, Anjali and Beena were all quite thrilled by this – they went on a cheerful shopping expedition to buy her the full kit: Barbie bag, Donald Duck crayons, Chhota Bheem water bottle. Then, only three days after she'd started, Anjali declared she didn't want to go to school anymore. "But why?" asked Mrinalini of Beena, whose disposition was growing more amiable by the day.

"I don't know, didi," she replied, apologetically.

"Did something happen? Maybe she's feeling shy."

"Maybe didi. There's a school function no, they have to make a dress."

"That's all? Why, we'll get her a dress! Tell her. When is it? I'll also come."

The function consisted of a small, cloth-covered stage and thirty toddlers in tears. It was a day of heat and high humidity; young fathers fanned themselves with the Sunday newspaper they'd brought along as young mothers darted backstage, in wilful violation of the teachers' commands. Only Beena sat still, in a middle row, chatting happily with her sister, who had arrived for the occasion carrying strings of flowers for their hair. "Won't you go see?" said Mrinalini, sitting behind them. "Is Anjali okay?"

"Oh didi," Beena laughed, "if I go she'll only cry."

Indeed, every maternal appearance backstage was propelling fresh and voluble fits of tearful panic, until, with no more ceremony than a squeal of static, Shakira's *Hips Don't Lie* began to boom over the audience, drowning wails and catapulting stray mothers to the edges of their plastic chairs.

One after the other, Anjali's bawling classmates were thrust onstage, each wearing their 'dress': a letter of the alphabet slung around their necks. This small concession to learning was effectively undercut by

Anjali herself when she ran to join A, B and C with a jumping cheerful dance, though being herself a Y.

Anjali was carried offstage by a large and pink master of ceremonies who resembled, to Mrinalini, an overpriced prawn. When allowed to emerge again, at her appointed time and place, Anjali glowered at the audience with fierce, unbending concentration.

Watching her there, her dark little body, her small shoulders held rigid between children double her size, Mrinalini felt a surge of protective energy that propelled her to her feet and made her call out, "Anjali! Look here!"

At the sound of her name, Anjali smiled an absurd, open-mouthed smile and Mrinalini waved, tears – absurd, too, and sentimental – beginning to form behind her eyes.

"You know," said Mrinalini that evening on the verandah where they were drinking tea as clouds gathered overhead and a breeze ruffled the newly revived grass on their small lawn. The scent of damp mud filled the air, and the sound of Siddhartha clipping his toenails onto the newspaper supplement spread across the floor. His phone sat blinking beside him.

"Hmm?" he said.

"If we're going to pay for her education, then the least we can do, I think, the least we can do is make sure she gets something from it."

"What?" said Siddhartha, not looking up from his left foot.

"I mean, what's the point of her going to some great school if she comes home and has no back-up, you know?"

"Arre, who yaar?" said Siddhartha, looking up and catching on. "Oh, you mean this kid?"

"Yes, well. Who else? Don't you think?"

"What?"

"Uff... don't you think that we should," Mrinalini took a deep breath, "that we should give her some back-up?"

"Sure," Siddhartha returned his attention to his nails.

"Because... it's not like her parents can, can they?"

"What?"

"Oho, Siddhartha! I mean, her parents can't help her the same way, can they?"

"I don't see why not. They're damn enthu."

"Ye-es. But damn enthu isn't good enough."

Siddhartha looked up. "Why?" he said with a

new vigour. "Abraham Lincoln managed, didn't he? Studying by candlelight and writing with coal. What's her problem?"

"He did?"

"Sure. And our Ambedkar also managed, same way."

"With coal?"

"I don't know with what. Sitting outside the classroom with chickens."

"Chickens?"

"Yeah, chickens."

"You're making fun of me."

"Never!"

"Anyway, whatever. We can't just wait for her to become a genius can we? Maybe it'll be enough if she just becomes a doctor or something. Gets through the IAS or something."

"Yeah." Job done, Siddhartha raised his newly manicured feet to the small table between them. "She has a way better chance, anyway."

"At what?"

"Arre, at the IAS. Way better chance than either of us."

"What d'you mean?"

"Don't you read the papers at all, sweetheart? Did

you notice how I didn't make it to D-School? So what was that? It's all reservations, and she's highly qualified, let me tell you."

Mrinalini paused, but then shook her head, refusing to be drawn away. "Anyway," she said, "that's not the point."

"Yeah."

Siddhartha smiled in a way that made her ask, "'Yeah' what?"

"Sure. If it doesn't fit, naturally it's not the point." Then, as she opened her mouth to reply, Siddhartha leaned back in his cane chair and smiled and said, "No, look, all I'm saying is: you're making her into more of a victim than she is. I mean, sure, she needs help; we can help her. But she's not as vulnerable as you think."

"Really?"

Siddhartha shrugged. "Yes. She'll be fine, don't worry."

"But Sid, you had to see the other kids in this Sing-a-Song party. They're all double her size. They all eat *double* the food she does. Every day."

"You said yourself she's a fussy eater – you said you can hear her mother running after her all day with her lunch?"

"Yes. But she's not eating ice-cream for lunch."

"Neither are those kids, are they? Did you eat ice-cream for lunch ever? As a kid?"

"But things are different now."

"Come on. And look at all the chocolates you keep feeding her yourself. She's just small. What's the Eng-lit word? *Petite*."

"Uff! Why're you being mean, Sid?"

"Okay, okay," he said, not laughing but in good humour. A gust of air rattled their cups. "Anyway, we're not going to go change her genes, are we? We'll help her. Chill." He said 'chill' with a slight American accent to make her laugh.

"That's all I was trying to say."

The garden grew dark under the shadow of rolling clouds, leaves scurried in the air like an audience looking for seats in a suddenly-full theatre. Any minute now, the first fat drops of rain would fall.

Beena came out to clear the plates, Anjali trotting beside her, bursting with urgent news. "A ghost is come!" she said, putting a hand on Mrinalini's and looking straight into her eyes. "A ghost is here!"

"Ghost? Where?"

"Look," she said, her eyes wide, pointing at the storm about to break "a ghost is come!"

"Of course not," Mrinalini laughed. "There's no ghost here. Who's telling you about ghosts?"

She looked up at Beena, but Beena had turned and was walking away with the tea things.

"There *is* a ghost."

"*Is* it? Then where does it live?"

"It lives…" she scanned the garden, "in there it lives!"

"In that tree?"

"In that tree. It doesn't fall!"

Since Siddhartha was always aloof in such situations – he patted Anjali's head, returned her greetings, gave her sweets even, but he never played with her – they were all a little surprised when he called to her now, "Come here, Anjali, tell me about this ghost!"

Anjali remained where she was, rubbing against Mrinalini's knees.

"Come here?"

"Go on," said Mrinalini, "go and see what Sid bhaiyya is saying?"

"Come on? Come, tell me about that ghost?"

Anjali took one cautious step towards Siddhartha.

"Show me? Where does he live, this ghost?"

Without taking her eyes off him, Anjali pointed backwards into the garden.

"There?"

She nodded slowly.

"Then, do you even know what to do if a ghost comes?"

She shook her head.

"You don't know?"

She shook her head.

"Shall I tell you?"

Anjali nodded, with guarded interest. Siddhartha bent in his chair towards Anjali. "You have to… eat it up!" He made a gobble-growling movement with his mouth. "Like this! Okay?"

She nodded.

"So what do you do, if a ghost comes?"

She shook her head; it was a game.

"You have to… eat it up!"

The fourth or fifth time he did this, Siddhartha emphasised *eat it up!* by tickling Anjali's stomach. She shrieked with laughter. When her mother came back, she said she would not go and it was only when the rain began to smash its way down from a black sky, flying into their faces, that they all got up, first to admire the downpour and then to retreat indoors.

Maybe it was the weather, the air suddenly soft and cool with water, but Mrinalini felt a desperation to be orgasmed that evening. Chhote Lal was in the kitchen, sizzling onions in his kadai as the pressure cooker whistled, Beena was in the quarter coaxing Anjali's dinner into the child, and Siddhartha was watching the news on TV, the remote held loosely in one hand, his phone in the other. Domesticity hummed a busy tune through the house walls. You couldn't help wanting to nuzzle into it, this soft and steady rhythm, with something naughty – muddy footprints on the carpet, a handful of sweet, shelled peas stolen from the kitchen counter, a short, breathless fuck before dinner.

So, Mrinalini changed into her softest, shortest, flimsiest nightie, bolted their bedroom door and knelt by her husband. "What?" he smiled. "Are you being a gangster's doll?"

"Moll."

"Moll. Or are you being Julia Roberts in *Pretty Woman* –"

"Moll."

"When he takes her up to the hotel and she says she won't kiss his *mouth*, but... you know."

"Moll!"

"Fine. Moll. Where's my tall glass of watery whisky, then?"

"Oh!" she brought a hand to her mouth. "I'll have to go out then…"

"No, no," he bent low and kissed her neck. "Don't *go* anywhere," he kissed her again and cradled the back of her head in a palm. "Do gangster's *doll's* usually correct the gangster's English?"

"Moll. Moll-moll-moll," she said.

"Right." He tugged gently at her head and she cried out a small 'no', but then she drew herself across his lap, letting her nightie rise above her thighs. The warmth of him growing beneath her contrasted nicely with the cool, damp air playing on her bare skin.

"What?" he said.

She wiggled her bottom in return; he stroked it. "Why must you be so bad?"

"*You're* bad," she said, "You're *mean* like a… like a hyena."

He smacked her and she gasped. "Don't be rude," he said.

Sure, Siddhartha was a banker, and he liked his bed-tea at 7.30 and his dinner at 9 and his Sunday lunch exactly ten minutes before 2, but that doesn't mean he couldn't make Mrinalini come. He loved it when she moaned, and he'd do anything to make her. Dress up, tie down, shower and spank; play with ice-cubes and dance naked and sip chocolate from her thighs and tease her for long-lasting minutes until she cried.

She wiggled herself up to sit astride him. He pulled her face down to kiss it, she reached for the button of his cargo shorts.

"Badi didi! Badi didi!" A small weight fell against the door, tugging at its handle. "Where's badi didi?"

On Siddhartha's lap, Mrinalini jumped a little and sat up straight. He looked at her and muttered, "Damn."

"Badi didi!"

"Shh! Anju, wait!"

"Badi didi, open the door!"

"Didi's working! Come here, Anju!"

"Haan!" Siddhartha called, much louder than he needed to. The timber of his voice made her almost a little scared, though it seemed to have little effect on Anjali, who continued pulling at the handle and calling for Mrinalini. Now Beena, too, knocked hesitantly at the door, though all the while repeating, still, "Badi didi's working Anjali, don't disturb her!"

"Haan!" Siddhartha called again, throwing his hands in the air, reaching for the remote and raising the volume on the TV. He turned to Mrinalini, who was going to let them in, and said, "At least, change?" before crossing his legs and fixing his attention on the news. She rolled her eyes at the back of his head, then went to the bathroom for pyjamas.

When she emerged, Siddhartha was unbolting the door. He'd only half-opened it when Anjali squeezed her way through and ran up to the middle of the room. Looking about in wild excitement, she caught sight of Siddhartha first and then her breath, and folded her hands in a namaste so demure that, despite herself, Mrinalini laughed. "Namaste!" she replied.

Anjali looked this way and that. "Where's your TV?" she asked.

"My TV? The TV's right there, see?" Mrinalini pointed across the room.

"That's not your TV. Where's *your* TV?"

"That's not here. Don't trouble badi didi," said Beena, reaching out to take her daughter's hand.

"Oh! You mean my laptop? My computer?"

"That's didi's computer, Anjali. It's for work," Beena looked at Mrinalini and smiled. "She saw the cartoon yesterday, no? Since the morning she's been saying, I'll watch TV with badi didi."

"Has she, really?"

Despite everything, Mrinalini was rather pleased. She hadn't thought that Anjali remembered her when she wasn't around. Mrinalini brought out the laptop, invited Anjali onto the bed and, having cajoled Siddhartha into turning off the TV, began to look for a suitable cartoon.

This wasn't a particularly difficult assignment: Anjali was devoted to the moving picture. What took time, really, was finding videos suitable for Anjali's enjoyment. Hindi film songs, though certain to please, were dismissed on the grounds that they were not only crass and lewd, but also ubiquitous. Anjali would find them for herself soon enough, she needed no guide to Bollywood. The cartoons that Mrinalini skimmed through were either too violent or too inane – or, "let's be honest," as Mrinalini said to Siddhartha over dinner, "too much in English. She has no idea what's going on, and how'm I supposed to explain to her why a fat panda wants to learn Kung-Fu?" Clips from National Geographic, though entirely worthy, were often too long. Half-way through, Anjali was pressing at the keyboard or stabbing at the screen, saying, "We'll watch cartoon?" in her most brisk and optimistic manner.

Today, though, they had barely started browsing when Mrinalini clicked on a bhajan by mistake. This was an old favourite of Jahanara's that Mrinalini had got into the habit of listening to every few months; a scratchy old recording of *Maiyya mori* in which Krishna, butter-handed and butter-mouthed, explains to his mother, pleads with his mother, grows angry with his mother, saying he never ate the butter, he never would, he never could – how can she love him and say he did?

Anjali wriggled, but Mrinalini didn't like to interrupt. "Listen," she said, "listen, he's talking to his Mama, his Mummee." She raised the volume and Pandit Omkarnath Thakur's deep old voice filled the room like a live thing, mournful and magical, playing with the tune as a small child might with a large dog – fearless.

"Listen," she whispered, "close your eyes and listen."

How could I, says Krishna, bundled before Yashoda by the village, all clamouring for his punishment. He shakes them off. *I was out with the cows all day! When would I eat any butter? Don't believe them, what stories they make up! Why would I steal any butter?* But there is butter on his face, butter on his hands, butter on his breath. *Fine then, fine! Everyone knows I'm not your real son, you'll believe anything of me – go ahead, do what you will, I'm running away!*

But then he cries. *Maiyya...* softly, *Maiyya...* weeping, *Maiyya...* so innocent and injured and alone, *Ma....*

Mrinalini opened her eyes and saw that Anjali's mouth was open and her eyes were full. Shyly, a little awed, Mrinalini reached for her hand and held it till the bhajan had played itself out.

Mrinalini was so pleased by this accidental success that she allowed them to proceed at breakneck pace through The Three Little Pigs, the travails of Donald Duck and similar entertainments, until they found themselves watching an animated life-story of Baby Ganesh. Anjali's eyes lit up. "Ganesh ji!" she said, delighted, and sitting up straight she folded her hands and bowed her head. "Do Namoh!"

"Haan," said Mrinalini, taken aback and a little embarrassed, "You do… do your Namoh." She glanced at Siddhartha, who had returned his legs to the coffee table and was reading the week's *Outlook*. "That kid is cute, okay," he said, not looking up, "but she's drowning in hair-oil, I can smell it from here."

"Uff, Sid."

"I'm just saying… keep her away from the pillows."

She sighed at this, but without rancour; and when Beena walked in, she, too, smiled to see her daughter's head resting on Mrinalini's shoulder, and Mrinalini smiled back, casual and loose-limbed.

"Dinner's ready," said Beena and Siddhartha said, "Okay, let's go."

"Come," said Mrinalini, still smiling, "come see what your daughter's watching." Beena walked tentatively into the room and stood beside them.

"What are you watching, Anjali?" she asked.

"Ganesh ji!" Anjali did not take her eyes off the screen, nor did she shift her weight off Mrinalini's shoulder. "Ganesh bhagwan!" Mrinalini craned her neck to look up at Beena; mother and daughter had the same smile: willing to be pleased, then delighted. "See," said Mrinalini, "it's a cartoon. Sit?" She wasn't sure where Beena would sit and counted on her declining the offer, which she did. They were like this a few moments, Mrinalini and Anjali prone on the bed, Beena half-bent over them; both mother and daughter entranced by the screen. Mrinalini began to feel the effort of not moving her limbs. When Siddhartha rose and said, "Chalo then, are we having dinner or what?", Mrinalini propped herself up gratefully and lifted the laptop off her knees onto the bed. Anjali leaned towards the computer as her mother put a hand on her back and said, "Come Anjali? We'll watch the rest tomorrow, okay?"

"No!" said Anjali, pushing at her mother with both hands, frowning at having to turn her head from the story for one torturous second.

"Come along," said Mrinalini, and she reached forward to pause the video. "Come, we'll have dinner and you can watch later, no?"

"Want to watch now," said Anjali more beseechingly, and then, with sudden inspiration, "You go and have dinner, okay?" She tilted her head to one side in an imitation of cuteness that Mrinalini was half-repelled by. To undo the effect, Mrinalini tilted her own head at an exaggerated angle and said "Okay!" just as Beena said, "No, Anjali, we have to go now. Dinner's ready."

"No!" Having found an ally, Anjali pushed again at her mother who caught her hands in hers.

"Don't do that!"

"No! You go!"

Mrinalini looked up at Beena with a conciliatory smile, "It's okay, let her watch." She turned back to Anjali. "You'll sit here alone and watch?"

Anjali nodded vigorously. "You'll not be scared?"

To this, Anjali did not deign to reply. "Okay then. I'll go have my dinner, you watch. But don't break anything, okay?"

"Okay," said Anjali, and Mrinalini nodded at Beena, who smiled again, but a little tightly now and Mrinalini looked away.

As the three adults left the room, Mrinalini turned and said once more, "Don't break anything, okay?" but Anjali was too absorbed to respond.

When they returned, Anjali had fallen asleep, her head limp and her breath even as the cheerfully pious drama played on. Siddhartha clicked his tongue in exasperation, and she was relieved the head wasn't on *his* pillow. Not sure what to do, Mrinalini returned to the kitchen, as if nothing had happened, and said to

Beena, as if by chance, "Your Anju's gone to sleep", and Beena smiled a busy, distracted smile over the sink and said, "She's sleeping?" and Mrinalini said "Yes," and smiled herself in return until, having turned away, she wondered if her tone had conveyed that she was in no hurry to have her bed back, or if it had proposed that Beena could leave her daughter in her unpaid care for as long as she wanted, or if (she couldn't quite think this) it suggested she *liked* having Anjali asleep on her pillow – until she was no longer sure what she felt or should feel or even what she wanted to feel anymore.

Still, having committed herself to the holistic development of Anjali's mind and character, Mrinalini didn't discourage Beena from bringing the kid into the house with her. On the contrary, she dug out Siddhartha's dusty old toys, bought crayons and chart paper, and began to divide her evenings between playing hide-and-seek behind the thick curtains in the drawing room and watching Anjali pound out letters of the alphabet, one fist holding down the paper as the other manoeuvred a blunt pencil. She did this with such regularity and seeming devotion that eventually Siddhartha put the TV off and padded up to them in the study where he watched them struggle to tame the 'e' and then said, "You're really into this."

Mrinalini looked up and smiled.

"I mean… baby. You don't have to spend *all* your time on this – everyone can see how much you're doing."

"Aww!" Mrinalini turned in her chair. "Are you jealous?"

"No! I'm just saying we won't… I won't let anyone send them off. So you don't have to worry, that's all. And you're probably not getting any time for your book even."

"I know. I'm not worried, I like it. It's fun."

"Okay. If you're *sure*."

"Yeah. Sure."

"And your writing?"

"Oh, that… who knows? This is so much more real, you know?"

"Struggling against class privilege?"

"Yeah. And against horrid men who want to throw her at crocodiles when in fact, *look*: she writes the best 'e' *ever*."

"Hmm…"

"Say it's nice, Sid!"

Siddhartha said it was nice and then he kissed his

wife's head and patted the kid's and wandered off to the kitchen to ask what Chhote Lal was making for dinner.

Then, one day, Mrinalini found an old copy of *Dracula* in a cupboard and was just beginning to get really terrified for Jonathan Harker, and was therefore hardly capable of spending the evening admiring misshapen stick-figures. So, when Beena and Anjali arrived, she told them she was busy and promised to be free the next day. Unfortunately, though Beena took her daughter into the kitchen and installed her on a stool at the counter, Anjali had entirely failed to understand Mrinalini's meaning. She lowered herself off the stool and tottered back to Mrinalini's room, approached the bed on which Mrinalini was reading her book, and said, "Come?"

"Oh. No, darling. I told you, I have some work to do today."

"Are you working?"

"Yes," said Mrinalini stoutly, holding up her *Dracula* as if it were a charm against bossy little kids.

"Come," said Anjali, obtusely, "let's write A-B-C!"

"*You* write, darling. Why don't you write A-B-C, and D-E-F, and show me tomorrow, okay?"

"Okay!" Anjali ran off and Mrinalini sighed, feeling both guilty and relieved. She could have saved herself both emotions; a moment later, Anjali was racing back in, flapping her chart-paper behind her like a flag and spilling crayons in her wake. "A-B-C!" she cried, pulling herself onto the bed, throwing up the remaining crayons and tearing a hole in the paper with her knee.

When Beena appeared to remove her daughter, Mrinalini waved her away; obviously, resistance was futile.

The following evening, Mrinalini found herself checking the time every few minutes. As seven o'clock approached, she felt a tense coiling in her stomach and decided to lock the door, pouring herself a double vodka and opening a new file on her laptop for good measure. She was staring earnestly at the ticking cursor on her helplessly blank screen when Beena knocked. Once-twice and she left, and Mrinalini was glad to hear her announce that didi was busy. She was about to breathe when Anjali's more urgent register rattled the door, her bang-pound-bang hurtling like a small dog through the room.

Closing her eyes, Mrinalini ignored it. "Mummee! Mummee!" called Anjali, "Open badi didi's door!"

"Come here Anju! Badi didi's busy no? She'll come in a little while."

"Where's badi didi?"

"Badi didi's coming Anju. Show me, show me your A-B-C?"

"No!"

"Come Anju! Badi didi will come soon. Won't you show Papa your A-B-C?"

"No!" shouted Anjali and there followed a vacuum of silence.

"That's not right," said Beena, "you shouldn't do that."

Anjali produced a small, enraged roar.

"Anjali!" Beena interrupted, "That's very wrong. Do I hit you? Does Mummee hit you?"

Anjali mumbled a response.

"Then? Should you hit Mummee? Is that good?"

Luminous fractals began to float across her screen as Mrinalini strained to hear more, but both mother and daughter's voices grew muffled and faded as they retreated to the kitchen.

Later, at dinner, Mrinalini asked where Anjali was and when Beena said she'd put her to bed, Mrinalini said "Oh" and tried to sound a little disappointed, to suggest they might have played now; but not *too* disappointed, in case Beena went and woke the kid up. All this cost effort and it was a strained and irritable Mrinalini who rolled Chhote Lal's pasta round and round her fork, feeling ill-disposed towards conversation of any kind and certainly hostile to the subject Siddhartha chose this night, of all nights, to raise.

"Good lord, no!" she said.

"Wow. That's very clear. But why not? I thought, since you're obviously so attached to this kid," he nodded his head in the general direction of the kitchen, "we might think… No?"

"No!" she breathed for dramatic emphasis. "Haven't we talked about this, Siddhartha? You agreed this wouldn't be an issue."

"I know, I know," Siddhartha put his hands in the air and leaned back in his chair, "I know you said you don't want to be rushed into having children."

"Or ever."

"Or ever, yes. We agreed to that. I wasn't sure myself if I wanted… but now, Leenu, don't you think it's time? I mean you're so *good* with…"

"You're asking me? Or this Leenu person? Some extra-marital floozy of yours?"

"Mrin-aaa-lini. Don't you think it's time we had kids?"

"Not at all, Siddhartha. I don't."

"Okay." And he shrugged, as if it wasn't such a big deal after all.

But the idea had obviously got into his head because some days later he tried again. "So, Mama sends you love."

"Oh. You spoke to her?"

"This morning, yeah."

"So what's the news?"

"Just the usual: she's worried about Gautam."

"You mean Andrea?"

"Yeah."

"Why does she worry so much though? He's not marrying her."

"Yeah, but he might. And you know what she thinks…"

"Of Andrea. Yeah. Though I have to say, on this I totally agree. That Andrea's no good. No good will come of her."

"Yeah. Tell Gautam."

"If I tell Gautam, he'll have married her before I hang up. He just needs some distraction."

"Hmm…"

"The *problem* is, you've just confused him, you know?"

"Confused him? How've I done that?"

"I mean, not you. Your parents, because now he thinks they're anti-Andrea because she's *black*."

"American."

"Yeah. Black American: how well up you are on the lingo, Sid."

"No no, *just* American. It's not a race thing, I told you. We think…" he paused, "*they* think it'll be easier for him, you know, in the long run if he's with someone from the same culture."

"Right."

"*Yeah*, right. What, now you think my family's racist?"

The 'now' was dangerous and Mrinalini decided to let it slide. They were talking in the car, and Siddhartha was never entirely happy behind the wheel, honking and snarling his way through the slightest jam. Sometimes she'd find herself holding her breath. So, now, she looked out of the window and let a moment pass. "All I'm saying is, *Gautam* thinks your opposition is…" she thought of the right word, "irrational. Whereas there are actually many *other* reasons to worry about her. I mean, like she's completely psychotic."

"Yeah!" he laughed, which took her by surprise. "So anyway, now she's got this other thing."

"What? To worry?"

"She's worried that we... that I..."

"Don't tell me. You're causing her worry? The apple himself?"

"Ha-ha. Not worry. She was just asking, you know. If we had any plans."

"Plans? To visit? What?"

"No. I mean to..."

"Yeah?"

"I don't think she'd mind being a grandmother," Siddhartha blurted it out before he lost courage. Mrinalini turned to him in her seat and said, "Oh, Siddhoo," in an almost pitying way.

"Yuck. I've told you a hundred times, don't call me that, please."

"Oh yeah? Did you say, '*Leenu* don't call me Siddhoo?' Maybe I got confused..."

"Ha-ha. But anyway, she was just asking, that's all."

"Then I hope you told her we're not planning any such plans."

"I said. Yeah. I said you're not interested. Just yet."

"Uff. Make me the villain, fine."

"Not the villain. It's true though… you're not interested, right?"

"Yeah."

"I know. But why not, though? Don't you think it'd be fun?"

"But we talked about this, we decided."

"I know, I know. But that wasn't a final decision. We decided no hurry. Thirty-three is no hurry, I'm sure."

"It is if I feel it is, isn't it? I don't want kids."

"Ever?"

"No! I don't know. Maybe some day. Not now, but. Come on, Sid."

"No, I just don't understand, that's all. Why not?"

"Because. There's so much else to do. I want to live, you know. To have adventures." She said it and she knew it was the wrong thing to say.

"Adventures? Like on a pirate ship?"

"Uff."

"Then what?" Honk! "What adventures?" Honk! "The *child* will be an adventure." Honk-honk!

She felt all her clenchable bits clench. "Cleaning

shitty nappies is not an adventure, Siddhartha, I can tell you that."

"I'll clean the nappies."

She shook her head. "No, you won't."

"I will."

"No, you won't. And who'll make the money, then? Kids need food and school fees and shoes."

"So we have money."

"Not if you're cleaning nappies, we won't."

"And by the way, Mrinalini, they make nappies *disposable* these days."

Triumphantly, Siddhartha manoeuvred his way past a dented Ambassador taxi hogging the right lane.

"Anyway," said Mrinalini.

"Yes?"

"Those are more expensive."

"God," he pulled back behind an overloaded truck, "we'll *have* money."

"Fine. Then we'll have even more money when we're thirty-six. Then we'll have children."

"At thirty-six? Why?"

"I don't know. Maybe I'll feel like it then."

"I see."

"Okay?"

"Sure. You just basically don't want to make any sense."

"If you want to put it that way."

"I do."

"Fine."

"Fine."

"*Fine.*"

She let him have the last word.

4

*Or leads, at its worst,
to a big old fight! fight!*

Chhote Lal's attempt on Harish's life could have gone two ways: relations between Siddhartha and his tenant Brajeshwar Jha might have been irreparably strained, or – as, in fact, happened – been turned to friendship. Having enjoyed each others' company through the crisis, each decided to try the other out in more peaceable conditions and they were soon regular invitees to each others' parties. Siddhartha always brought along a bottle of wine, while Brajeshwar proved himself an entertaining raconteur, if liable to drink a little too much and hug a little too close.

His favourite story was Aurangzeb's, and he always told it the same way, so Mrinalini had it almost memorised and would sometimes catch herself mouthing it along with him. When this happened, she'd move to another circle.

"So Aurangzeb," he'd begin, and it was the rare evening that didn't offer him the chance to. Any conversation, from the logistics of day-trips to Agra, to grim prognostications on the future of Islamic terror, would do. "So *Aurangzeb* was a funny fellow," lightly turning his glass to melt the ice against its edges and taking a sip, "and he was funniest in Burhanpur. And *Burhanpur* is a funny place I'll bet a month's rent you've never heard of."

If anybody had, he didn't wait for them say so. "Burhanpur is this tiny hole of a town in MP, *booming* red-light area now for the district, but three hundred years ago? It was *the* place to be: the Mughals almost made it a second capital, *that's* how important it was; Mumtaz Mahal was buried there, *that's* how important it was."

Now, he would pause, and inevitably someone would frown in concentration, and someone else would say, "Isn't that…?"

"Yes. Shahjahan's Mumtaz. Died there, 1631, spawning her fourteenth kid, who was screaming in the womb they say, all most ghoulish and terrible. They had to bury her where she died, right? And she'd still be there if it wasn't cheaper to get marble to Agra, which is why they dug up her skeleton years later and put her in the Taj, where," if there were white people present, Brajeshwar would point his cigarette at one of them, "people like you get to pay a fortune."

The foreigner would grin woefully. "Go to Burhanpur, my friend. It's free. *And,* the exact same place she was buried? That's were Aurangzeb wooed this girl he fell madly in love with, Hirabai Zainabadi, winsome courtesan but no easy lay. I mean, not only was she his *uncle's* favourite concubine – which is anyway tricky – but she was giving him no patta, nothing. And who can blame her, right? What if she succumbs and next day he's pushed off to conquer the Deccan, what's the uncle going to say, right?

"But Aurangzeb was damn persistent; running around trees for her, staring deeply into her eyes, so she devised a test."

At this point, he'd stop and glance at his glass. Someone always offered to get him a refill.

"The test is this, it's the test of all times: Okay, you love me, then prove it, right? Aurangzeb says, *Sure, of course,* just tell me, I'll kill a tiger, I'll climb a mountain...

but Hirabai, she just holds up her hand and – *ta-da!* – she's holding a big fat goblet of wine.

"But Aurangzeb's hard-core fanatic, right? Wine is total fuck-no defilement. So he looks at her and she's holding this poison out for him and he knows he's going straight to hell. Then he looks at her again: her eyes are shining, her bosom is heaving and he shakes his head and he says *Fine. Give me that goblet.* Snatches it from her, closes his eyes and he's raising it to his mouth and the brim is just reaching his lips and then…"

"Then?"

"Well then she snatches it right back. No need, she says, you've proved your love."

Always, there was a moment of silence before someone laughed – Ha! – and said, "That's a good story."

Mrinalini, meanwhile, was pleased in a dubious kind of way to discover that Brajeshwar was writing a novel too; sometimes, when he came down with the month's rent, they'd sit at the dining table, drinking coffee and planning to take the literary world by storm. If the one made it, he or she would keep the door open for the other, because they knew how these things worked: how talent is shut out, or it drowns.

In fact, this spurred her to open her own Word files more often, though currently these contained only bits of arbitrary prose interspersed with inspirational quotes she'd found while Googling 'how to write a novel'. To sit down every evening and tap out a few lines, knowing that Brajeshwar might well be tapping out a few lines upstairs too, that at any minute they might emerge in triumph, showering page upon page of heart-thumping, bestselling *story* upon the world – this gave Mrinalini a sense of belonging to a larger cultural workforce, and of deserving her dinner, both of which were gratifying sensations, particularly in light of their plummeting account statements.

Though Siddhartha had made comforting calculations that proved they could live a year on his savings alone, and often remarked that households of four and six functioned happily on his Young Advisor pay, the fact was it wasn't enough. It barely covered the electricity bills and the servants' salaries. Of course, they'd known they'd have to economise. They'd have to serve Smirnoff at their parties not Grey Goose, and stop picking up boxes of pink Australian grapes just because they looked pretty – but these things are hard to remember, if your hand reaches out where it used to and your brain isn't wired to make approximate calculations of the bill before the cashier hands it over.

So, less than halfway through Siddhartha's experiment with meaningful employment, they had run through rather more than half their joint account, and Siddhartha began to read out news of price rises – onions, petrol – in a meaningful manner. Rattled, annoyed and more than a little aggrieved – it wasn't *her* idea, after all, to go around chucking up perfectly good jobs – Mrinalini redoubled her efforts at the laptop, but the more she tried the less it all made sense while ever greater grew the temptation to play just one more round of online Scrabble.

The house was thick with tension, and soon a small spark blazed into the biggest fight they'd ever had.

Nobody in the neighbourhood could tell how it began because, naturally, it didn't begin as audibly as it ended, but not even Mrinalini and Siddhartha, who were there throughout, were ever entirely clear about the fight's origins.

It could have started in one, or several, of many ways. Perhaps Siddhartha complained, as he had begun to complain, of a fan left on in some unoccupied room. But that is too literal, too direct an opening. More likely, he came home from work and lay down on the bed where Mrinalini was hunched over her heavy, black laptop – his first anniversary present to her, and one she now wished she could exchange for a Mac. Turning on his side, Siddhartha reached for his wife, her arm perhaps, or her stomach, maybe he let his hand rest on her left breast and said something like "Can't you find another time for this, Leenu?" To which, perhaps, she snapped, "Don't call me Leenu."

He may have moved closer, kissed some part of her, said, "What shall I call you then, writer memsahib?" and she would have pushed the computer's lid shut and opened her eyes wide and said, "What?"

He might have tried, he might have asked her, "How was your day, then?"

"Rubbish. As usual. How was yours?"

And maybe this is when the fight began, when he smiled and said, "We had a party. That Lakshmi Sood is going to get married, remember? They got sams and jalebis, the works, and her Shivlal Sir made a little speech – what a speech, I tell you. *Lakshmi* will be celebrating her Diwali soon, I should say! We will be missing her cheering face *till* the time she returns… but job is job, I say, and marriage is marriage." Siddhartha would have laughed, "Job is *job*, and marriage is *marriage*!"

If, at this, Mrinalini made a face and refused to smile, Siddhartha could justifiably have sat up in bed and said, "So what? You're superior because you don't make money or cook?"

"I don't like cooking. *You* cook if you love it so much. And I don't even like money. Not like you, not like some *worshipper* of money."

"Oh really?" a moment away from pacing the bedroom, "Oh really? You'd be happy, sitting on the streets? Nobody'll give you a –" he shook his head from side to side, "nobody'll give you a laptop when you're begging at some traffic signal, you know. Nobody'll give you crispy lamb dry on a *tray* you know."

At this, she would have delayed losing her temper, giving him time to recant, to realise his foolishness, his cruelty. She was only doing this for *him*. "Money's not real Siddhartha. It's not like water or cotton or even your stupid jalebis. It doesn't *mean* anything, it's just a concept, it's just paper."

"Oh really? Really? I'll tell you what's just paper, that thing you're scribbling, that's just, actually... ha! That's not *even* paper."

That would be when the screaming began, and the evening routines of neighbouring households were both enlivened and suspended for a fraught twenty minutes. "I cannot bear it any more, your *stupid*, boring life and your *stupid*, boring friends, and your, your, patronising attitude towards *every–single–thing* I do or think!"

"Oh, is that what you cannot bear? Shall I tell you what I cannot bear? I can't bear *you*! Sitting all day, doing no work and… and getting *fat* from eating all that shit you buy with my –" (he said it like a rap star, spreading his arms wide) "*mona-ey!*"

"Take your fucking money, I don't want to see one paisa of it, all right? Take your fucking money and live in your fucking house and eat your fucking bhindi and go… go *dance* in your big fucking office, all right? I don't give a *fuck* –"

There was the sound of glass, of bottles and metal vases and ceramic ashtrays smashing on the floor, on the walls, against the iron bars on their windows. Their voices were lost in the shatter, like the swirling *whoosh* of a storm is drowned by pouring rain. The front door was violently opened, violently shut: Mrinalini's voice rose clearly through the night air, "I don't need your house, I don't need your money, I don't need *you*!"

And he followed behind and he said, no longer shouting but with an angry shake in his voice, "But please, but *please*, be my guest, carry on, go write your Booker prize, go live in some ashram, go drink some ginger-lemon tea on some organic farm with some Israelis, okay? Please, please, go.... Go drink *Whitehorse* with your *Jahanara*. Be *happy*."

She swung the main gate behind her so it only just missed Siddhartha's head. She walked past an old man and almost fell on his sleepy old Labrador on her way to the main road.

It was only once she'd left the colony that Mrinalini stopped to consider her options, limited as these were by the fact that she'd left both wallet and cell phone behind. A cycle rickshaw hurtled by, startling her into tripping backwards and falling down. As Mrinalini looked up for help, the driver called out harshly, "Can't you see?" Nobody stopped; scooters beeped at cars that flashed their lights and young men in tight T-shirts strode by in small groups, laughing. She burst into tears.

How long she wept on the filthy pavement she couldn't say, but eventually Mrinalini's grief was interrupted by the persistent honking of a car across the road. Her misery now compounded by alarm, Mrinalini ignored the sound and buried her head in her arms. The honking stopped, ominously; a car door opened and slammed shut. Now she would be abducted and raped and hacked to pieces – that was all she needed. She got up, but her legs hurt. She'd never be able to run away. She felt a body behind her and turned, preparing to scream.

"Mrin – Mrinalini!"

"Oh," said Mrinalini. "Jahan?"

"What's *happened* to you? Are you okay? Mrin?"

"I'm fine." Oh, she was so happy she could cry. She did. Some more. "I'm fine," she sobbed, and Jahanara put her arms around her, careful not to let their bodies touch, "Shh, Mrin. What happened? It's okay… shh…"

In the car, wiping her nose on her sleeve, Mrinalini said she could not live with Siddhartha any more and Jahanara said nothing. So often had she fantasised about rescuing Mrinalini from a doomed and loveless marriage that to find the scene set for her like this left her dumb with stage-fright. She whispered a few more *shhs*, until Mrinalini slipped some sudden inches down her seat and cried, "Drive, drive!"

"What?"

"He's here! Look! He's coming!" And there, in fact, was Siddhartha, half-running in shirtsleeves and pyjamas out of the gate. "Drive!"

Jahanara drove. She took them home, a few minutes away, and parked outside her own gate. "Did he see us, do you think?" Mrinalini had wiped her cheeks with her palms. "Idiot! *Let* him suffer."

"Mrin…? Did he hurt you? What happened? You shouldn't run away from him… we'll confront him. Come in, tell me what happened."

They slipped from the front door to Jahanara's bedroom. "Do you mind," she said, a little shyly. "The parents are having some dinner, so it's full of people outside."

"No, of course…"

"It's why I'd gone out actually, avoiding the aunties, you know."

"Yeah. Sorry Jahan… I dragged you back?"

"No no! Don't be silly… I'm just glad I found you. You looked so… god, Mrin, what happened?"

"I don't know. We had this terrible fight and he said such *things*, and I don't think I can ever… he's just so *mean*."

"Yeah?"

"Yeah. I mean, he's the one who quit his job and I'm only trying to help, you know, just help… I totally supported him even though he's making *no* money now and suddenly he wants me counting tomatoes in the kitchen, and hoarding light bulbs and… and making *babies*. He's got this obsession…"

"Yeah?"

"Yeah. I wish I could be like you, you know. No strings, no stupid *social* expectations all the time…"

"Well…"

"No really. You don't care what people think, how you live, what you do…"

"Well… I *do* actually plan to move out with Geeta."

"Geeta?"

"My… you know."

"Oh! Well you should! That's great, Jahan!"

"Yeah, well. She's one of those 'space' people."

"Oh yuck. I hate those people…"

"Yeah. What do they need all that space for, right? I mean, what're they doing, building an expressway?"

"Ha, right. Yeah."

"Anyway."

"Yeah…"

"So listen, you're welcome to stay, if you like. There's, um… there's a room and everything."

"Thanks Jahan. You're such a *hero*."

"Oho, no." Jahanara felt herself blush and turned away. "But you're always welcome, you know…"

Mrinalini reached for Jahanara's hand. "Thanks, Jahan. Really. I don't know what I'd have done today, without you. And I know you didn't have to… you don't have to," here she laughed, "you don't have to even *like* me."

"Don't be silly."

"But it's *true*. I'm a *terrible* person – nobody should like me!"

"Uff Mrin. That's not true. Of course I like you."

"Oh Jahan…"

"Mrin, it's okay." She had on her driest voice, but what with Mrinalini's eyes filling with tears again, it wasn't easy.

"Oh Jahan!" With this and no warning, Mrinalini flung her arms around Jahanara, buried her damp face in her neck, and there was nothing Jahanara could do but stroke Mrinalini's hair and whisper, "Shh…", as much to her weeping ex-love as to her own madly beating heart.

It was a while before they were settled again, and Mrinalini was laughing at herself – "Just *look* at me, I'm making *scene* after scene!" – and Jahanara was laughing, too, but only from fear and happiness, and then Jahanara said, "Well? D'you want a drink?", and they both remembered why they were here.

"God, yes. I'm just so angry… and he goes on about how I won't cook as if it's some *sin*, you know. I can't eat if I don't make my own stupid gobhi, it seems."

"Gobhi, yuck! At least you should make gosht. Wait, actually, let me get you something… it's a full Mauzee-dawat tonight."

"No, no, Jahan, don't go! What if someone comes in? They'll see me like this and think you've picked up some beggar person from the street."

Jahanara looked her up and down. "With that little diamond nose-ring? Don't think so, Mrin. Anyway, I'll be back in a second."

In fact, Jahanara was away almost twenty minutes, greeting assorted relatives, and when she returned, holding out a platter of kebabs, she found Mrinalini sitting cross-legged on the bed, playing with her hair.

"Okay?"

"Yeah!" Mrinalini dropped her hand, guiltily.

"Here. Try this one first… it's the family special."

"Oh wow! But I can't eat all of this!"

"No, just try this one…"

Mrinalini tucked a bite of beaten meat into her mouth and swallowed. "Wow, Jahan. This is yummy!"

"You like it?" she smiled. "You're actually supposed to eat it with this special roti, the chap's just bringing it…"

"No, listen Jahan, don't worry."

"It's no trouble."

"No but listen, I just… sorry I should've asked. I just used your phone. I called Sid."

"Oh."

"Yeah, sorry… he'd just panic and then he'd call my parents and *they'd* panic and so I…"

"Yeah, of course."

"I just… he's just coming to get me."

"Okay."

"If I'd known you had kebabs…!"

"Right. He's welcome to join us...?"

"No no! You were going out anyway, I won't…"

"Yeah, well… I can have this packed for you."

"No…" the phone rang and Mrinalini snatched at it. "Hello?"

Jahanara turned and began to walk out of the room. She was at the door when Mrinalini called out from behind, "He's here."

"Okay."

"I'll go then…"

"Yes, of course." Jahanara carried the platter still, and Mrinalini followed rapidly behind. When they reached the main door, Jahanara insisted Mrinalini take the kebabs with her. "With my compliments," she said. "Just don't break the plate on his head: my mother'll want it back."

Mrinalini laughed and reached out to hug her, but Jahanara stepped back an inch. There she remained until she heard the squeak of the gate open and close, the growl of a departing engine, and then she pulled the door towards herself very gently till it shut.

5

Since everyone must *have their pride*

They made up in style. Siddhartha carried her into the house as she shouted "But I'm fat, I'm fat!" and then he spent an hour in penance, on his knees, kissing her ankles and massaging her buttocks and nuzzling her vagina until she shouted "Come, come!" and he said "I'll make your world spin, baby" and she was upon him, gingerly turning, and it was funny and awesome and they were sweating and happy and crying and burnt with desire all through night and morning and all the way into the week which he took off and flew them to Goa where they ate discounted crabs and made loud falling-lampshades kind of love until it seemed that life was only this: a short and aching bliss.

When they returned, it was too soon. It felt wrong to wake up for work and eat daal for dinner. So, to extend the feeling of holiday a while longer, they planned a party.

Jahanara came with Geeta. They were the first to arrive, and Mrinalini was still getting dressed when the bell rang. When she hurried to the drawing room, she found them looking up at a painting of a tiny, stick-figure fisherman tumbling on the high seas, his line taut and his arms tensed against his catch, far and deep below him in the invisible dark: a fish many times the size of his rickety little boat.

Jahanara's arm was curled around Geeta's bare waist and for a second Mrinalini wondered what Siddhartha's banker friends would make of this and then she said, "Hey!", stressing the cheerful exclamation mark.

They turned together, and smiled.

"We got that in the Philippines," said Mrinalini, taking in the sight of Geeta's long, bare midriff, breasts squeezed into a bright blue blouse, the whole wrapped loosely in a peacock-green sari.

"It's lovely," said Geeta. "Hi!"

"Hi, hi!"

"This is Geeta; Geeta: Mrinalini."

"Hi!" They laughed. "I'm sorry, Sid's not here. He's just gone to the booze shop. It's a disease: every time we have a party, half-hour before it starts he's convinced we're going to run out."

"Oh no, no problem. We're early anyway. We should apologise."

"You're not early, you're…"

"On time?" said Geeta, dryly. "It's the worst Delhi sin. We should be denied all paneer at dinner."

There was a small, only slightly awkward pause. Jahanara laughed tentatively. "Nice walls, too," she said, gesturing with one hand. "Last time I came –" she glanced at Geeta.

"So!" said Mrinalini brightly. "Drinks?"

"Oh no, we'll wait."

"Wait for what? You're here, the party's started!" She was walking to the bar when Beena came in, Anjali stumbling in behind her at her toddler's trot.

"Didi? He says to tell you the kebab has come." Anjali stood on tip-toe, reaching for the phone in Mrinalini's hand and Mrinalini hoisted her up in her arms. "Look who's here," she said. "Who's this? Jahanara didi!"

"Say namaste!" said Beena, smiling.

"And Geeta didi!"

Anjali shook her head at the two women, watching them intently.

"Hello!" said Jahanara, and to Mrinalini, "I thought you didn't even like children?"

"Yeah. Not to have. Say namaste, go on."

"Namaste, indeed."

Mrinalini laughed and bent her head close to Anjali's ear. She made a tickling noise and Anjali pulled her head away, not quite smiling. Mrinalini did it again, and patted her tummy. "Where'd you get this frock?" she said. "It's very pretty!"

"It's my frock," said Anjali. "My frock."

"Accha? Give it to me then?"

"She got it for Rakshabandhan," said Beena.

"Who did you tie Rakhi to, haan?"

"Bhaiyya!"

"Who bhaiyya?"

"*My* bhaiyya!"

Mrinalini turned to Beena who explained, "My sister's son."

"Ah! Your bhaiyya! Then give it to me?" Anjali shook her head. "It's not your frock," she said.

"Accha, is it not?" her arms hurt and she deposited Anjali back on the floor. "Go help your mother, then. And Beena? Tell Chhote Lal to heat them properly before sending them out, okay? Not like last time."

"Yes, didi," said Beena and was leaving when Mrinalini called again. "Oh Beena?"

"Yes, didi?"

"I wanted to ask. Is everything okay in her school?"

"Oh yes, didi. Everything's fine."

"Tell me when her crayons finish. I'll get more."

"Okay didi. She breaks them all, what to do?"

With a small shrug, Beena left while her daughter announced, one last time, "It's *my* frock."

Mrinalini turned to her guests. "She goes to this school, Sing-a-Song," she explained, as casually as she could. "I'm teaching her the alphabet."

"Oh?" Jahanara seemed interested if not yet impressed, and Mrinalini would have been glad to elaborate but the bell rang and Siddhartha's voice filled the room. "I've got the beer," it announced cheerfully, "and look what I've got with it!" Then there he was, a carton in his arms and behind him Brajeshwar in a blue beret, a bottle of wine in each hand. "Hello Mrin Singh," he said. Then, seeing Geeta and Jahanara, "You started without us!"

It was hardly a shock that Brajeshwar found Geeta attractive – some girl at every party suffered the fate – so when Mrinalini passed by and heard him dust out a new story for her, she stopped, not really thinking anything of it, but hoping only to be amused.

"Okay, well Guru Dutt's *first* film I'm sure you've never seen: *Baazi*."

"Sure, yeah, *Baazi*." She had a slightly nasal way of speaking; it gave everything she said an ironic sheen.

"Oh," said Brajeshwar, clearly deflated.

"No, well, I haven't seen it, actually. Go on?"

"I just saw *Pyaasa*," said Mrinalini, for no particular reason, knowing how Brajeshwar hated unchoreographed interruptions.

"Ah," he said, looking at her with both eyebrows raised, like a librarian at a ringing cell phone.

"Yeah," she persisted. "Didn't like it though. For a *poet*, he's quite *fat*, no?"

Jahanara laughed. Encouraged, Mrinalini added "I mean, not at all like a poet who's been bypassed. More like a poet who *needs* one." She grinned broadly at her audience, but Brajeshwar shook his head, grunting. "And you want to be a writer."

Mrinalini was opening her mouth to object but he'd already returned his gaze to Geeta. "Anyway. So *Baazi* introduced, for the very first time to Indian cinema, guess who?"

Mrinalini raised an eyebrow in what was, she hoped, an ironic indication of the deepest disinterest, but nobody was looking at her.

"Okay," said Geeta, "I don't know this one. Who?"

"Badru."

"Badru?"

"Yeah. Who's Badru, you're asking? Well, Badru was this guy, forever bugging Balraj Sahni for a role, right? And Balraj Sahni had written this film, *Baazi*, and he *wanted* to give Badru a role – wanted him to play a drunkard, in fact, but he wasn't sure how to get the others on board, right?

"So what he does is, one day they're all sitting in the office, Sahni and Guru Dutt and Dev Anand – who was starring in the film – and there's this massive racket and this *damnably* drunk fellow barges in and he's just talking all this shit to Dev Anand, slurring and toppling and everyone's falling over themselves laughing, right? So finally, they decide they've had enough and let's just chuck him back out onto the streets, and they're about to carry him out when Balraj Sahni says, 'Hey, Badru! Say hello.'"

"Surprise, surprise."

"Yeah. It was Badru all along. But you wait for your

surprise. So immediately, right, *immediately*, Badru's stone-cold sober and super genteel and everyone's just stunned. 'Wow', you know."

"And he got the role."

"And he got the role. And he got a screen-name. Which was Johnny Walker."

As if despite herself, Geeta laughed.

"Surprised?"

"Okay," she said. "Yeah."

Since nobody seemed interested to ask whether *she* was surprised, Mrinalini smiled tightly and slipped away to get a drink, telling herself she would avoid Brajeshwar for the rest of the evening. This she might well have done, but the more she tried to ignore him, the more she couldn't help notice his pursuit of Geeta, no more than she could help being irritated by it. So, eventually, Mrinalini returned to their little group, where Jahanara stared into the middle distance as Brajeshwar punctuated his stories with friendly pats on Geeta's arm, and dragged him out for a smoke.

"So," he said, without preamble, "that Geeta's hot, huh?"

"Do you *really* think so!" she widened her eyes. "Because from the way you've wrapped yourself around her, nobody can tell."

"Ha-ha." He raised his glass and drained it. "Don't tell me you're jealous?"

"Please! But you should know she's not…"

"What?"

"She's not interested in you."

"Oh please. She is loving me, *bay-bee*."

"No, she's not."

"She is *only waiting* for me to make my move. In fact, it's her I should be out here with now… What'm I –" He turned to go and she called after him, "No, Braj!"

"What? Oh come on, Mrin Singh. Don't be such a bore, yaar."

"But…"

"But-but-but. No but, just bet, okay? I'm going in there now, you'll see her at breakfast, and then you'll owe me a plate of Chhote Lal's pakoras. Now let me go, Mummy-ji."

She might have continued even then, but it wasn't as if *You want to be a writer* hadn't rankled. She had her pride. "Fine," she said, raising her cigarette to her lips. "Bet."

He grinned and hurried away and she could tell he thought he was charming, and it was hard, seeing how much he believed it of himself, to disagree. It was almost guiltily that she watched him teeter through the French windows towards Geeta and Jahanara, talking to each other in a far corner.

It was a pratfall in slow motion. Maybe the two girls had decided something between them, because it wasn't long after Brajeshwar joined them that he seemed to straighten a little and laughed self-consciously and made a big show of draining his glass, holding it upside down for them to see. He was still laughing when Geeta leaned across and whispered something in his ear.

At this, Brajeshwar turned his glass back up, nodded briefly and began to walk away. Something in his long face had crumpled and Mrinalini took a step back into the verandah, not wanting to catch his eye.

As a result, Mrinalini's feelings vis-à-vis Brajeshwar were already quite mixed when he came down a month or so later, bearing not the rent cheque but a hardcover emblazoned with his name.

"You never told me!" she cried, standing on tip-toe to hug him.

"Aah… it's hardly anything."

"Shuttup! You're not going to be all jaded with this!"

"No," he grinned and his delight was apparent, "it *is* pretty cool, right?"

"Yes!" She hugged him again, for no particular reason, and said, "Wow, Braj. You did it! And how, when... I didn't know you'd even finished – when did you even get the time?"

"Oh, you know. Evenings... just spare time, like that."

"Wow."

She did truly admire him then, and invited him to come later when Siddhartha was home and they'd have a proper drink. But later, when he'd gone and she sat down at her desk with his book and began to flip its pages, Mrinalini was surprised by a sudden rush of pain and self-pity, and she had to close her eyes and tell herself she was happy for him and smile broadly into the dark to make her body believe it.

After a few minutes of this exercise, she was able to pick the book up again and, turning to a page at random, she started to read.

Caste is fraught. In our fly-infested Community Centre, it is as fraught as anywhere else, so it's no surprise that eventually the subject came up and started telling me its story. In this case, it arrived in the form of a dark young student of Political Science (of course) who came up to me one day, of his own free will and volition, dressed in the kind of shiny, tight-fitting T-shirt favoured only by the very poor and the very ironic.

Rakesh – that could easily have been his name – was intrigued by my gathering of urchins, thought I was a social worker and wondered if he might approach me for a job or some such form of livelihood assistance. Once disabused of the idea, he hovered anyway, with such persistence that eventually I sent the kids back to their begging and invited him to have a cup of coffee with me at the local Coffee Day.

Rakesh was obviously impressed that I was writing a book, and delighted to find me, like him, a Bihari. I was delighted to find a Bihari who wasn't mugging for the civil services. Instead he wrote poetry, part of an effort to demolish the elite Brahmanical order. At this point, I thought it relevant to mention that I'm a Brahmin with no wish to be demolished. To this he replied that, no, he and his fellows didn't want every single literal Brahmin to be ground beneath their feet but that some would certainly benefit from such treatment.

We parted amicably, with much felicitation of each other, and to be honest I'd have been happy to never see the man again. His poetry sucked.

But woe the ethnographic life. Rakesh had my number and he used it. At first, I didn't mind. With two pegs of Old Monk inside him, my new friend was a self-propelling motor. "Arre bhaiyya! These fuckers. I don't mean you, of course, you're a true, a real intellectual, but these fuckers, don't ask me. Today one fellow says we are living in a 'post-caste society'. I said, you're living inside

138

your own asshole, bhai. Look around. They've made Mayawati 'reactionary', that is the latest. Arre, you can't take it if a Dalit has a handbag? Every Dalit must wear torn pants with torn pockets, because two coins clinking is also accumulation of capital? Fuckers…"

This was enough amusement for the odd evening, and if Rakesh had merely confined himself to ranting against (general) Brahmanical hegemony while admiring my own (particular) self-indulgence – what else to call it, after all, this writing of books? – our association might have grown long and deep. Sadly, it soon became apparent that Rakesh's admiration for my project was only secondary. In the first part, he wanted to become its central focus.

Every time we met, he had a new tale of inhuman atrocity to relate. His grandfather had been burnt alive for digging a well. His maternal uncle, the first in either family to achieve a salaried position, that too in one of the lower echelons of the government, had been suspended for corruption, creating a kind of history since no one in the department – or, in fact, the tahsil – had ever faced such an outlandish charge. In college, Rakesh had been forced to drink his own urine.

It was when he told me that his girlfriend of two years was leaving him because he'd finally told her his full name that I began to think he was making a lot of this up. First: I'd known him almost six months and he'd never mentioned a girl. Second: he showed neither guilt nor shame in drinking down the money his suffering parents sent him. And third: his PhD proposal had been accepted by a university in Berlin; so what was the man complaining about?

Anyway, the next time I was having a drink with my landlords, I brought up the subject. Simran and Raj, always more circumspect in their judgments than I am, are particularly careful about caste. Watching them choreograph a balanced view between them was like watching an NRI introduce a white girl to green chutney: Oh no, no-no, that's too much, just touch a little to the tip of your tongue and keep the water close – you'll see what I'm talking about!

Simran couldn't say what she was more aghast at – Rakesh's plight or my insensitivity. She told me a long story about watching a man climb down a shitty drain to unblock it. Raj interrupted to say that caste had been hijacked by profiteers and wasn't it entirely possible that Rakesh was stalking some girl who didn't like his face, not his surname. He warned us against getting emotional. Simran said yes, patriarchy was even more entrenched than caste, but damn not getting emotional. We owed our privilege to others' sufferings and she thought it was a writer's primary duty to expose injustice. Raj said injustice was having to wonder whether any of our children would ever get into a college without a reserved seat. That's what we should think about, not some lumpen's failed romance. Simran thought such bourgeois concerns shackled empathy, but Raj felt you could be empathetic without being patronising – India was littered with crutches and anyone – anyone who wanted – could stand up and walk.

In any case, they both said to me with a kind of pity, if I was going to be involved I should be responsible. Everything is not a joke.

Then, three days later, I got a call from a hospital.

The girl had a brother – patriarchy 1, Raj 0 – who had friends. Together, they beat the shit out of Rakesh. Specifically, they broke both his legs, a few of his ribs and all the fingers on his right hand.

The worst part? (Raj 1, empathy 0) he *had* been stalking the girl. At any rate, his love for her was hardly requited. The Dalit revelation was a pity card. He thought she might love him for sociological reasons.

Final score: minus-ten grand. I paid his hospital bills.

Having read thus far with horrified fascination and ever-widening eyes, Mrinalini now wrenched her gaze from the page and flung the book at the table; it landed with a thwack and lay there, coolly superior. How could he, thought Mrinalini. She thought it in italics with a question mark and exclamation both – *How could he!* and then, in a lower tone, How *could* he?

When she thought about it, she didn't know where to begin. To have written a book was bad enough. To come sauntering down with a copy of a book he'd written and someone had published *in hardback* was bad enough. And then, to *then* say he wrote the book he'd come sauntering down with 'in his spare time'. In his spare time. Mrinalini thought she might laugh; in fact, she thought she would; she did. It made her choke. What had Brajeshwar *except* spare time; in her head she posed the question to Siddhartha. What did he do *except* be overpaid to... to do what exactly she didn't even know! And what did it mean 'spare time'? So casual, so off-hand – had he written between meals, in traffic, sitting on the *pot*? No doubt.

Turning away, looking through the window at the dusk gathering outside, Mrinalini shook her head from side to side, a movement that loosened unwept tears, which began to trail down her cheeks.

She wiped at her face with the palms of both hands. Why should she cry if Brajeshwar was a lying, backstabbing, mean-minded... *crow*. He wasn't even any good; he was nothing but an aspirator, an aspirant, a puff of air lost in the wind. A briefly contaminating fart.

Had Mrinalini and Siddhartha been anything less than generous, friendly, kind? They had been *really* very nice to him. And now to do this, turn them into his little joke. Raj and Simran indeed. Did he think a sentimental movie reference would somehow make up for...

When, an hour or so later, the doorbell rang, Mrinalini sprang to her feet. She had to stop herself from rushing to greet Siddhartha with a copy of the offending book; instead, she blew her nose and poured herself a small vodka, which she swallowed neat before settling down before her laptop and opening an empty Word file.

"Hey darling."

"Hi!" She could tell her voice sounded unnaturally high and enthusiastic.

Siddhartha stood at the door, letting it be abundantly clear he wasn't coming in, so as to not disturb her while she worked. But now she wished he would; that he would see the book and say, Oh, what's this?

"Working away?"

"Well…"

"I had the most ridiculous day. Head's throbbing."

"Oh!"

"Yeah, well. I'll just go shower I think."

"Okay, but…"

But he'd turned and the door was closing behind him. The thought of waiting another fifteen minutes for him to emerge from the bathroom filled Mrinalini with a kind of panic. Snatching the book from the table, she hurried behind her husband shouting, "But have you seen this!"

He turned, reluctantly. "What?"

"This!" she waved the book at him, and waited. It took Siddhartha a moment to register the title, the author's name, the whole meaning of it, so he said "What?" again, and then "Oh, it's out?"

"What?"

He looked at Mrinalini, his mouth half-open. She blinked. "You knew?"

"Knew what?"

"That he's published this –" she didn't know what to call it.

"Yeah. Everyone knows he's been writing, what's the…"

"No, but I didn't know he'd gotten a *publisher*. Did you?"

"Oh! No, no…" he turned again, resuming his way bath-wards as Mrinalini, still holding the book out into the air, began to fear a horrible fear. "You did!" she called after him.

"No, no, Leenu. How'd I…"

She ran to overtake him so she could look at him. Siddhartha couldn't lie. When he tried, a comical, sheepish look filled his face. "You knew!" she said, blocking his way.

"Of course not!" But there it was, the grimace, the downward tug of the lips, the eyes rolling away from her. She wouldn't let him pass until finally he laughed a little and said, "Uff. Fine. He told me. I don't know why he didn't want to – I think he wanted it to be a surprise. For you."

"A surprise ? Why? I'm not his mother, what do I care?"

"Well, I don't know. Ask him."

"But… did he tell you also," the idea had all the light, unreal quality of a sudden dizzy spell, "did he also tell you about this… *Raj* and *Simran*? Did you *know*?"

"Oh." Again the downward smile. "You don't think that's cute?"

"Cute! You knew!" She didn't know what to react to first, "But he's making *fun* of us Sid! Have you even read it?" She knew, as she asked, that he had.

"Arre, look he just showed me a page or two and I thought it seemed okay. I mean, I didn't think it was a big deal – we argue all the time, it's not a secret, is it?" He reached out to touch her arm and she pulled away.

"Yeah, sure, of course *nothing* is a secret it seems,

145

between you two bum-chums. I mean, all the secrets are just from *me* it seems!" She raised her arms and her eyes to the ceiling as if calling to God. Siddhartha, taking advantage of this momentary shift of focus, slipped into the bathroom. "My head's a bomb," he said, from safely within, "Let me shower, okay?"

Minutes passed. Mrinalini realised she was standing and staring at a closed door. She turned and walked slowly back to her study, feeling the book cold and smooth against her palm, and poured herself another vodka.

* * *

"Leenu?" She heard him walk towards her, smelt the talc on his body pressing into the room's still, cool air. He put a hand on her shoulder. "Sweetheart?" and, pulling the pin from the grenade, "Are you all right?"

She was so angry the words stuck in her throat. "Yes," she managed, "I'm fine."

He sighed. There was no earthly reason for him to sigh so loudly. Since this was clearly a deliberate provocation, and it was uncomfortable to be half-turned in her chair, craning her neck up to look at his frown, she snapped, "What?"

"I just, um…" said Siddhartha.

"What is it, *Raj*? Shall we go milk a cow in our mustard field?"

He walked around to face her. "You're really upset. Why, sweetheart?"

She twirled both her hands to show him they were empty. Look: no reasons. "I don't *know*. Could it be that you lied to me? And that your best buddy *Brajeshwar* is making fun of us for the whole world to see in his *really bad book*?"

Siddhartha nodded. He had a peculiar way of nodding, like a spring in his neck had been loosened and needed to go through a series of diminishing movements of uncertain number before coming to a sudden halt. Now, it made her skin curl.

"I'm sorry," he said. "It was just silly. I should have told you."

"Yes! And you should have asked me, *Brajeshwar* should have *asked* me if he could just *write* about me and give me stupid names from stupid films!"

"Yeah. I guess so. I think he just thought, you know…"

"What?"

"Nothing."

"What? What? Why are you making excuses for him?"

"No, I'm just saying," Siddhartha spoke with two fingers across his mouth, trying to stop the words as they left him. "I think he thought you might feel…"

"What? Feel what?"

But Siddhartha had given up. "You know, sweetheart, I think competition is a good thing. It's good to be competitive. You know?"

"What're you *saying* Sid? Who's competing with who? What would I feel?"

"Nothing. Leenu –"

"What 'Leenu'? Tell me? What would I feel?"

"Darling…"

Mrinalini shook her head and turned it to face her computer. "I'm working."

"I'm sorry," he said, but she knew he could see the blank screen. "Do you want to be alone, then?"

"Yes!" she said with greater force than she intended, smacking the desk so her palm hurt.

"All right," Siddhartha began his slow nodding again, "But listen, it really wasn't the way you're thinking. Brajeshwar just wanted to surprise you and I just…

you know I've been working late. I just didn't think."
He waited a moment, then began to walk away.

"No you didn't," she called after him. He stopped and turned, "What?"

"You didn't just 'not think'," she imitated the false, simpering tone of his voice by, for no particular reason, swaying her upper body from side to side.

"Listen," he took a step towards her, but she held up a hand to stop him.

"You thought very much. You thought it all *through*. You thought, you and your *best friend*, you thought you would think up the best way to make *me* think and… and feel like worthless, stupid *idiot*," she continued to sway, getting up and waving her hands in the air. "You thought it would be a great *joke*, to turn me into a cartoon, to *humiliate* me – that's what you did!"

"Mrinalini?" He frowned a frown of fake, rotting concern.

"And then you come in here to see if I'm 'okay', if I haven't hurt myself in my little game that I play, running around my little study, if I haven't tripped on my, *tripped* on the table's fucking legs!"

Siddhartha raised one hand, oh he was the fucking Buddha now? "Calm down," he said, "calm down."

"*You* calm down," she yelled, "you calm down," she raised the book in one hand, "and *you* leave me alone!" – and she hurled it at his head.

Siddhartha walked carefully through the door. Then, unexpectedly, he banged it shut. For the briefest moment, this pleased Mrinalini, then it scared her. She strode towards the door, tripping on a small table, kicking it away as she steadied herself so it crashed into a cane bookshelf, unsettling the vodka bottle, which shattered on the floor.

Mrinalini tugged open the door, intending to bang it herself, louder and better, to bang him *out*, him and everyone – and saw that Anjali was looking up at her, with mouth open and eyes wide. They stared at each other a moment. Mrinalini felt the anger retreat from her eyes. Carefully, she lowered herself to the floor and reached out to touch Anjali's cheek. The child moved away.

This was more than Mrinalini could take. Tears rushed to her eyes, her stomach heaved, and before she knew it, Mrinalini had burst into exhausted sobs. Immediately, Anjali set up a reciprocal howl until Beena came hurrying and took her away in her arms. Siddhartha was less prompt, but eventually he, too, returned, and finding his wife so crushed and damp and salty, he relented. Attempting an awkward embrace, he exclaimed "Darling!" and "I'm sorry!" – which only made things worse. As Mrinalini gasped for air, Siddhartha tightened his hug, so it was a while before he could fathom, through Mrinalini's breathless moans, that she wished him to go away and leave her alone. This, after a brave attempt at stroking her hair, he did.

In the hall empty and silent, Mrinalini leaned her head against the doorjamb and forced herself to breathe, and breathe, until she hiccupped.

6

*When damning reviews creep
too close to home,*

It was as if Jahanara was galloping through the internet on a white horse, boldly decapitating a Brajeshwar-headed Ravana. With the light of the computer screen shining in her eyes, Mrinalini let out a sigh of pure pleasure, the kind you breathe halfway through a book so good you don't want it to end. Smiling to herself, she scrolled to the beginning and read the whole thing again.

Let me just say it outright. There may be a way of cheating your brain into imagining that Brajeshwar Jha's *Underbelly* is ironic, or empathetic, or in some way – any way – written with some sensitivity to context and fact. You can try all you want – I certainly did – but the fact is, for all that this 'ethnographic memoir' has drawn praise for its 'refreshing' take on caste, class and religion in modern India, the book and its author betray a troubling mixture of brazen arrogance and, worse, indifference.

So we are presented with Naresh ji, an ageing, cataract-ridden guide in the forgotten central Indian town of Burhanpur. Unfortunately for Naresh ji, his watery eyes disgust Jha, as do his worry and his gait ("swaying side-to-side like a girl"). So, when Naresh ji makes the mistake of confessing a mistrust of Muslims, we know he's had it. A few pages later, Naresh ji reveals another weakness – he has a 26-year-old unmarried daughter – and Jha turns the full wrath of his secularism upon him:

"Naresh ji!" I said, "what have you done? Why did you delay so long, haan? Now what will you do? No pension also, and all her fussing also, how do you think you'll manage? What were you thinking?"

Naresh ji turned his head, a half smile playing with the weak muscle of his face.

"It's a big mistake you've made, Naresh ji. What mannat will help you now?"

"Sir!" he began, but I'd had enough.

Perhaps there is something soul-satisfying in this crushing of Naresh ji's Muslim-baiting spirit. There is even a setting sun, later, that frames it all in just the right tinge of heroic grandeur. But even so, something doesn't ring quite right, and I don't mean the pathetic wimpiness of Jha's opponent, but the mystifying silence of the only actual Muslim in the whole chapter.

Khalid bhai is the driver, but he does little in these twenty pages except smoke cigarettes and grunt. If Jha is so keen to reveal the deep truths of Burhanpur – a Muslim-majority district in a largely Hindu state ruled by the BJP – then why doesn't he spend a moment or two talking to a Muslim? But no: Naresh ji must be allowed to chatter on and on, burying himself ever deeper in self-confessed communal tendencies, until he is soundly swatted by our hero, who then walks triumphantly into a sunset as we all exhale our *wah-wahs*.

But, you say, isn't Jha motivated by good intentions? No doubt, but we all know where good intentions lead: and Jha's subsequent encounter with a young Dalit boy is nothing short of hellish.

Let's begin at the beginning. What exactly does Jha mean by saying that Rakesh the Dalit studies political science and composes anti-Brahmin poetry, 'of course'? Is that a joke because, ha-ha, Dalits are interested in politics and protest? By all the couscous in Khan Market, why should they be? Wouldn't it be so much more pleasant if they took up another kind of hobby, a useful craft, some soul-satisfying seva?

But no. Not only does he write poetry, he writes poetry that 'sucks'. We have only Jha's word for it, of course; and again, we must trust Jha when he tells us that Rakesh can't possibly have suffered any great privations because he's received a German grant. I was, at this point, almost too stunned to continue. This may be news for Jha, in whose rarefied world foreign grants are the apogee of ambition, but a trip to Europe does not wash away centuries of exploitation. To have achieved such a grant must have cost Rakesh more courage, determination and hard work than Jha can either proffer or imagine.

Next, we encounter Jha's well-meaning landlords, quite

obvious foils to Jha's Brahmanical (he iterates his caste several times) benevolence. Trapped in that most stodgy of political categories, 'landlord', and mouthing self-serving neo-liberal fears or shallow platitudes, they offer him at least one bit of advice he should have taken: "Be responsible".

It is too much, though, to expect Jha to understand the meaning of the word. Sure, when Rakesh is beaten senseless, Jha pays the hospital bills. And with such clever, cynical, po-mo verve he does it too! But does he once visit Rakesh after he's discharged? I'll bet you my copy of *Annihilation of Caste* he doesn't.

I just hope someone doesn't start calling for *Underbelly* to be banned. Because then we'll all go haring off on our little freedom of speech debate, muttering ritual incantations to a constitutional provision that, all alone it seems, will keep us from tumbling into the gloomy, orc-ridden castle of Mordor. Let us, by all means, allow Jha to speak. But please, let us not mistake his drunken dinner-party anecdotes for deep thought.

After her second reading, now feeling almost sorry for Brajeshwar, Mrinalini decided to send him a message asking if he'd like to go out for that congratulatory drink they'd never had. Brajeshwar agreed with a cheerful enthusiasm that had vanished when Mrinalini walked into a neighbourhood resto-bar to find him glowering at his soup.

"You read it?" he asked, almost before she had sat

down. As if, thought Mrinalini, mentally rolling her eyes, everyone in the world was only following his news.

"Um..."

"Idiots," said Braj, deploying his spoon with such force that soup splashed upon the tablecloth.

"What?" Mrinalini frowned. "Why're you drinking soup?" She looked sideways and smiled at a waiter hovering a few steps away. "What is it?"

"Please," Braj swallowed a mouthful and let his spoon clatter against the plate, "please don't insult me by pretending you didn't know. Is that what this meeting is about? A let's-all-be-friends session?" He raised a hand and called, "Excuse me? One large Black Dog!"

He didn't ask what Mrinalini wanted and she had to call after the waiter as he turned, to order her vodka and tonic. She tried again, "So, what…"

"Don't 'so-what' me. You and that man-hating banshee of yours! Don't act like you don't know!"

"Braj! Listen, I don't know what you're talking about. *What* are you talking about?"

"You're really going with that defence?"

"I don't know what I'm defending myself *against*."

"You really don't know?"

"I *promise*. I do not know. What is it? What happened?"

He stared at her until their drinks arrived, and took his first sip without breaking eye-contact. Then he turned. "*God.* I *hate* this stupid no-smoking law!"

Mrinalini exhaled. "Yeah." She drank some vodka and said, "So… what happened?"

"What happened? That lesbo *bitch* of yours *happened*. God yaar. Why didn't you tell me she was psycho-insane, Mrin? I mean, if she wants to write deep and probing characters sketches, let her try to *do* it, bhai. If she's too weak for any real writing, then please, let's not have her given free range to smother us with her fucking insight in a thousand fucking words!"

"Your voice…"

"Fuck my voice!"

Mrinalini held up her hands. "If all you're going to do is yell at me, I'm going out for a smoke." She half-rose and Brajeshwar tried to smile but it came out distorted. "Did you read it?" he asked, in a lower tone.

"Wh –" Mrinalini began, then "No," she said, clearly and definitively, sitting back down. "But I gather it's something no good. About your book?"

"What else? Fucking dyke."

"Well. What'd she say?"

"What did she *not* say? I need another drink. You done?"

"Sure."

"You know what it's like?" said Brajeshwar, holding his second whiskey and leaning across the table at her. "You know, it's like I got married, right, but I don't have a human, actual bride. It's like the book is my wife, and I have to take it around everywhere and –"

"Defend its honour?"

"Yeah. And then people, all these uncles and aunties, they all gather like vultures, you know, and they all want to know, 'What next? When's the good news?'"

"Ha. You can't make 'good news' with a book, Braj."

"Sure you can. You can get an American publisher. Or you can get a Bollywood producer. And then, instead of *any* of that, what *I* get is your –"

"Not *my* anything."

"I'm just saying, look at the state of *thinking* in this country!"

"Well…"

"No, it's not what she wrote about me, okay? What

I mean is, why in the world did she *suddenly* decide to write about me? You know?"

Mrinalini said nothing and took another long sip of her vodka.

"That's how these things work. It's not like she wants a real debate. And who… who writes blogs anyway? It's like you can't get any real paper to publish you, so you just type out whatever shit you want lying in bed and picking your nose."

"Braj! Don't be crude."

"Don't tell me what to be! Tell that *bitch* –"

"All right, all right. It's just a review, Braj. Why're you letting it get to you so much?"

"No, that's the point. It's not just a review – it's like she got an axe and she's trying to chop my balls off and *mince* them into fucking keema for her kebab."

"Uff. Yuck."

"And the *thing* is, why'd she do it? I mean, it doesn't even seem *ethical*, you know. She knows you, she met me –"

"I don't know," said Mrinalini, doggedly noncommittal. "People disagree…"

"This is not people disagreeing. I mean, just *read* it…"

"Okay, okay."

"I mean. Maybe it was my fault. I guess… I did hit on that trophy wife of hers. You think this is some jealous revenge shit?"

"Trophy wife?"

"Obviously, she must've gotten angry, right?"

"Braj…"

"And I didn't give it to her. I mean, it's obvious."

"What'd she want? What're you saying?"

"Oh come on! I mean, it must have hit some nerve. Maybe that trophy… maybe *Geeta* realised what she's missing and now your bitch-dyke can't stand it."

Mrinalini laughed. "You're saying Geeta likes you?"

"Yeah, well, sure. It's not impossible, Mrin. Women do. Especially…"

"But she's –"

"Please. She's just not been laid in years. It's obvious."

"Is it?"

"Of course. I mean read her crap review – can you imagine her in bed? It'll be all 'Oh!'" – he assumed a falsetto, "'Oh, let's not have orgasms because they're so *patriarchal!*'"

"Braj. She's not like that."

"As if you know." He held his empty glass in the air and ordered a third round. "She's obviously craving something real, you know."

"I don't think so."

"Yeah. Or wait, you know what? I have it! You know what she wants... she wants babies!"

"Shuttup, Braj!"

"But it makes total sense. Look at me: fair, Brahmin, can't complain about height. Haan?"

"Rising literary star?"

"Sure. Exactly. But she couldn't have me and now she's taking it out on the dyke who can't oblige, so then she puts on her demon face and tries to rip my –"

"Shh! Please, not your balls again."

But this made them both laugh, and when Mrinalini got home, more than a little drunk, she couldn't tell exactly whose side she had taken; whether she felt triumphant any more, over Braj, or just a little guilty about Jahan.

Her head buzzed at the light in the lobby; and Anjali, charging out of the kitchen with a hot frown on her face, seemed like an agent of shame.

"My Mummee is in the kitchen," she declared with no preamble.

"Yes," said Mrinalini, feeling the smile stuck to her face. "Your Mummee is in the kitchen."

"*You* are not anybody's Mummee!"

"Of course I…"

"You are *not* a Mummee!"

"I…" Mrinalini started again, but there was a brutal spite in the child's expression that made her want to slap her – it – and a small shiver ran its way through her skin. "My…" she tried again, but Anjali was staring at her so fiercely that all she could do was move her head in what might, or might not, have been a nod of assent.

She thought, after Anjali had run back to her parents in the kitchen, of following her there and telling her she could be a Mummee, a dozen *kinds* of Mummee, any time she wanted; she imagined Beena's embarrassment at her daughter's indiscretion and this helped, a little, to soothe her – but by then she had walked into her bedroom, and finding it devoid of Siddhartha she lay down on the bed to smoke an illicit cigarette and then, instead, she fell asleep.

She woke at dawn, all tucked in. Siddhartha had even remembered to slip the earrings from her ears, and unhook her bra. She slipped it out of a sleeve, tucked it under her pillow, and turned on her side to watch him sleep, feeling a great surge of love for this man, her caring, careful husband. Perhaps that woke him, because his lashes fluttered and he half-opened his eyes, looking at her, letting the fact of her gaze travel through his half-conscious brain, closing his eyes and opening them again, awake, asleep, awake, asleep, awake and he smiled. She smiled back, cupped a hand over her mouth and blew.

"Stinky," she said and he laughed a small, sleepy laugh and they looked at each other some more and fell asleep for another fifteen minutes, and then they woke.

"Then?" he said.

"Then?" she replied.

He opened an arm for her to slide on to; his morning bristle tickled her nose. "Nice time?" he said.

"Yeah," she replied without thinking, drifting this way and that on a warm sea of sleep. "Okay," she said, feeling it come back to her, letting the thoughts form. "Bitch-bitch-bitch."

"Hmm?"

"Such an aunty, that Braj."

He smiled the way people smile when they don't

quite get a punchline, and began to say something but she fell asleep again, into dreams of hungry reptiles, and when she really woke up the phone said 9.17 and the shower was running.

Siddhartha emerged, his favourite blue towel wrapped around his waist and his hair neatly combed; Mrinalini had propped herself up on both their pillows. "Hi," she said.

He made a sound, half-exasperation, half-laugh, as he stretched his arms one by one into a shirt and began the slow, deliberate process of buttoning up, a process so familiar that Mrinalini could watch it and forget if her eyes were open or closed. Sleepy, trance-like seconds washed one into the other; he finished with the shirt and reached for his trousers, neatly folded on a chair, and with his back towards her – he remained oddly shy about this exercise – he unwrapped the towel and pulled on his pants.

Once decent, Siddhartha turned to face her with an expectant look on his face. "Want to know what's happening?"

"What?"

"I've been up all night."

"What, why?"

"Your precious Beena. She's got a mean streak, I swear."

"Why but… what happened?"

"Arre nothing, yaar. She refused to let this poor chap into the room. So he was lying in the verandah, killing mosquitoes."

"Better than killing Harish."

"Ha-ha. Great joke. Anyway, then he called Mama…"

"In the middle of the night?"

"Well, it's day there."

"Yeah but. He called her? Or she called him?"

He clicked his tongue in irritation. "*How* does it matter? Point is, he burst into tears, so then Mama called me and I had to let him in and he insisted on sobbing some more, and anyway, then I told him."

"What?"

"That she has to go. We can't have this daily circus."

"What?"

"So I told him to break the news to her first thing and sort it out and, of course, now he's disappeared and there's no tea."

"Don't look at *me*."

"God forbid. Anyway, I have far too much of the stuff in the office. Rivers of tea... So I'm going to go. Will you be okay?"

"Yeah, why'd I not be okay?"

"I mean with these dramatics?"

"The dramatics of the domestics? Oh! But," she remembered now, she was waking, "you can't get rid of her, you promised!"

"Yeah well. He's been with us..."

"I know, I know!"

"And have you seen the size of mosquitoes these days? Must've lost half a litre of blood."

"What martyrdom."

"Don't be mean, yaar," he came over and bent to kiss her goodbye. "I'll talk to him on the way out and see if they're okay."

"And the kid? Her school?"

"Call me if there's bloodshed."

"Sid!"

"Leenu, I have to go. I'll call you, okay? I'll explain."

Her legs dangling from the bed, she watched him walk out into the corridor, heard the main door open and close behind him, strained to hear his voice in the

166

drive, the coughing start of his engine and then he was truly gone.

Immediately, she had the feeling of being all alone in a big house that might be haunted. A few more minutes also made it apparent that no lemon-honey concoction was forthcoming, so Mrinalini got out of bed, picked up the *Indian Express* and headed towards the bathroom, hoping her bowels would move with the aid of yesterday's news alone. She sat there a while, growing quietly absorbed in an account of a scandalous murder in a Mehrauli farmhouse, but then her feet began to fall asleep, so she flushed as quietly as she could and returned to the sleep-filled comfort of the bedroom, which smelt a little of Siddhartha's talcum and deo and invited her to bury herself in sheets still cool with the air-conditioner, an invitation she would have accepted gladly were it not for the urgent rumblings of her stomach.

The kitchen was many degrees warmer than the bedroom and Mrinalini stood before the open fridge for longer than necessary, letting the cool air flow towards her. Eventually, she picked out a pear, sliced it standing at the counter and was carrying the plate back to the bedroom when Chhote Lal shuffled in.

They avoided eye contact. He mumbled a greeting and she nodded, not quite stopping on her way, but when he brought in her glass of lemon-honey water a few minutes later, she said "Thank you", which emboldened him to ask if she'd like an egg.

In fact, Mrinalini had decided she'd head out. The atmosphere at home wasn't conducive to writing, certainly, and she feared the rising heat of the afternoon would inflame rather than stupefy tempers. Still, now that Chhote Lal had initiated a conversation, she felt she might add something of her own to it. "How's Anjali?" she asked.

"Okay, didi."

"She must be feeling very… hot, I'm sure."

"Yes didi, poor thing."

"I hope she doesn't fall ill?"

"Didi, Memsahib has said to give her coconut water… I get some every day."

"That's very good. I'm sure…" she was going to say she was sure there'd be no dearth of coconuts in the village, but decided against it. "You can bring her in here. If it's cooler here, you know."

"Yes, didi."

"Bring her? She can play here… or sleep."

"I'll tell her, didi."

"Haan, go bring her. It'll be good for her."

"Haan didi."

Mrinalini persisted. "The room is still cool from the AC. She can come…"

"Haan didi. I think she's giving her her bath now."

"Accha. Well, tell her anyway. I'll go out in a while, but let her come anytime, okay?"

"Okay, didi. Thank you."

"Okay."

For herself, Mrinalini had planned a long afternoon at the comfortably furnished and wifi-equipped Costa Coffee in GK II. She had heard of writers who spent whole days ensconced in those faux-leather armchairs, tapping away in inspired frenzy at their MacBooks, and the notion appealed to her. Plus, there was the undoubtable economy of free air-conditioning.

On her way out, laptop bag slung across a shoulder, car keys and dark glasses held loosely in one hand, Mrinalini called to Chhote Lal, "Accha, I'm leaving. I'll be back by about 4 – you'll make something for dinner?"

"Yes, didi." He emerged from the drawing room, holding a duster with an expression of due diligence.

"And listen, did you tell her? Let Anjali stay here, if you want, tell her."

He said, "Yes didi," and it was quite clear he hadn't conveyed the offer.

"Arre! Go and tell her! Go… I'll just come also."

Leaving him to drag himself out, Mrinalini went into the kitchen for a glass of water. She waited a minute for them to converse, allowing herself the small fantasy that, who knows, maybe this would be the beginning of a reconciliation, and then followed Chhote Lal into the driveway.

The quarter's door was closed – foolish idea in stuffy weather – and Mrinalini stood a moment, debating what to do. The low mumble of Chhote Lal's voice filtered through the wood and since Beena seemed to offer no audible rejoinders, Mrinalini thought there was no harm in hurrying the process along a bit, and raised her hand to knock.

As if on cue, Beena spoke up.

"Bastard! Drunken bastard! So easy to fall at your bhaiyya's feet! So easy to get rid of me! Murderer! You think I don't know what you're planning! What does it seem to you? I don't know what your plan is?"

If Chhote Lal tried to interject, he wasn't successful.

"You think you'll get rid of me so easy? Bastard! Only you can talk-talk to your memsahib on the phone? Who *gave* you that phone, haan? Get rid of me, keep your money, then what-what – you'll get a new woman? You think it's so easy? Falling here and there from drinking! Do you have any shame left? Any izzat? Bastard, say, why are you silent now? Shall I give you the phone to cry into? What stories you told! Putting me to work, giving your daughter as a toy to your owners! Haan?

"And your great didi! What, she can't have her own, so she'll snatch at mine? Whenever she wants, Anjali come here, whenever she wants, Anjali go away – and you show your teeth like a monkey! Did you tell her, who will pay this month's fee? All forgotten after two months of playing no? You and your didi – what a jodi!"

Mrinalini, her legs paralysed and her cheeks burning, might have stood there indefinitely if an elderly neighbour hadn't shouted across the wall in tones as stentorian as Beena's were wild. "Quiet!" said the voice. "This is a shareef area, not some mohalla! Quiet!"

Startled out of her daze, Mrinalini turned and hurried to the car, started the engine and realised the gate was closed. *God*, she honked a sharp beep-beep beep-beep *bee-EEP* – until Chhote Lal emerged from the garage at a clumsy trot, filling the rear-view mirror. "Coming, didi, coming!"

She didn't look at him as she drove out and it was only when she was out on the main road that she stopped in a small spot of shade to let herself blink.

Feeling almost ill with anger and mortification, Mrinalini picked up her phone and scrolled through names but it was just that kind of day: Jahanara didn't answer.

Do you choose good or bad, or merely all right?

Because she didn't want to come home a second before Siddhartha, and because the lingering strains of Beena's voice in her head and the relentless cheer of Costa Coffee's choice in pop music were combining to make her anxious, Mrinalini went shopping. She spent more than she'd planned to, so she drove home feeling as defensive as she'd felt driving out, and half-prepared, should Siddhartha say anything at the sight of her bags, to tell him to please and kindly go back to his banking because there was only so much one mortal person could bear... but as it turned out, Siddhartha was in a great mood.

He looked at her bags and then at her and grinned

and said, "So I hope there's some sexy undies in there, because you are going to want to pleasure me tonight."

"Oh yeah?" she said, dropping her bags and reaching to hug him in relief. "Why's that?

"Because I'm your hero."

"My Siddhoo!"

"Don't kill the moment yaar." He kissed her hair, gently. "So guess what?"

"What?"

"I spoke to Mama."

"Okay…"

"I mean, about this domestic situation."

"Oh." Her excitement deflated, and she had to stop herself from making a face.

"And I told her how you feel… how *we* feel about the kid and her education and all that. So she had this idea, and I think it's a good one, you'll like it…"

"Okay."

"That kid is going to turn three soon, right?"

"I guess."

"Well, Mama's saying, let her apply to some schools, good schools, and if she makes it, then that's a good reason for them to stay. I mean, it's worth it. But if she doesn't… then she might as well go back. She can always return later."

"Oh."

"You don't sound so excited."

"No, I am, I am. But, I mean… this school business is months away. I don't even know when –"

"Jan. I checked. That's only three months."

"But what if they keep fighting?"

"So everybody fights. People do, right? Look at us…" he smiled. "I told Mama about our –"

"You didn't!"

"Just a bit. I told her it was all my fault."

"As if she believed you."

"Anyway. I told her we'll handle it."

"You did?"

"Yeah. And we will. It'll be fine: that kid will become a doctor *and* get through the IAS. You just see."

"Okay."

"So… that's great right? You want to tell them? I didn't. I thought you should since it's really your doing. They'll be thrilled."

"Okay."

"Leenu?"

"Yeah? No, it's great news. Thanks, my hero. Let me

just um…" she walked away towards the bathroom, "let me just put on my sexy undies first."

"You'd better."

She smiled at him as she locked the door, then scrunched her eyes shut and sat a full ten minutes on the pot with the lid down. The phone rang. She looked at it and cut the call. A moment later, it beeped. *Sry missd yr call. U OK?*

Stupid Jahanara. Why had she worried about what someone who didn't even bother to use *vowels* thought of her? *All okay*, Mrinalini typed back, hoping spelling and grammar would convey something of her murderous resentment. *Had only called to ask if you could help with school admission for our maid's daughter, Anjali. All sorted now.*

There.

Taking a deep breath, Mrinalini got up, shed her clothes and stepped into the shower.

When she emerged, the phone showed another missed call from Jahanara and a message. *Thats grt! Lt me knw wht u need! G nd I were at anti modi rlly. Gt lathi chrgd!*

Siddhartha was absorbed in the news, and she stood behind him, listening to how the Chief Minister accused of genocide had held an audience of Delhi University students jam-packed and spellbound.

"Jahan was there."

"Oh yeah?" he said without looking up. "Liked it?"

"No, outside or something. They got lathi-charged."

"Really?"

"She says."

"It's not on the news."

"She says they did…"

"Hmm…"

"What?"

"There was security. That's not a lathi *charge*."

"She said –"

"Let her say. People overreact."

"I guess." She put a hand on his shoulder. It was a broad shoulder, the kind you could cry on. She wanted to cry on it now.

"Hey," he craned his neck to look up at her, "you should tell them, haan? They'll be happy."

"Sid?" she scratched at the shoulder, a bit like a cat.

"Hmm?"

"You tell them?"

"Go on baby. It'll be nice if you do."

"But I don't *want* to."

He looked up again, and smiled. "Feeling shy?"

"Yeah."

"Okay," he rose and kissed her forehead. "Come then, I'll take you."

"No…"

But he had her by the hand now, and resistance was futile.

In the humid kitchen, Chhote Lal was gratifyingly pleased and bent to touch Mrinalini's feet when Siddhartha unveiled her as the agent of their reprieve; he called upon Beena, too, stirring in a determinedly deaf manner at the night's potatoes. "Have you heard? Anjali will go to a big school, all because of didi. Come here, touch her feet."

Beena approached with her eyes to the floor, and mumbled something indecipherable as she bent half way. Mrinalini, who could feel the sweat rising on her newly washed skin, reached for Siddhartha's arm and said, "Come, let's go now!"

"Okay, okay," and he looked again at Chhote Lal. "But you tell that child to learn her full ABC! They'll ask in the interview."

"Arre, bhaiyya, she knows it all – phattar-phattar it comes out of her mouth, I can hardly understand!"

"Then you also learn no? In your old age, do this at least."

Both men laughed as Beena returned to the stove and Mrinalini to the door, tugging at Siddhartha. "Okay, okay. Didi's feeling shy, see?" With one last chuckle, Siddhartha followed her out and, as he settled back before the TV he said, half to tease her, half from love, "What becoming modesty my wife has!"

But Mrinalini had hidden her face behind her phone and did not reply, neither to Siddhartha nor to Jahanara, whose message she read once more before pressing delete.

Passing weeks did nothing to alter Mrinalini's disinclination to do either Beena or her daughter any favours. There was, for example, Anjali's habit of wandering about the house, pointing at things she found attractive or intriguing – a colourful necklace, say, or the trumpet Siddhartha had asked for at fourteen and learnt, dutifully, to play for a year – at anything, really – their pillows, a chair, a pen – and asking who it belonged to. "Whose is this?" she would say, and "Whose is this, and this, and this?"

It was dangerous, too, Mrinalini discovered, to give in and exclaim, "It's all *yours*, darling!" because this was a claim Anjali took seriously. So it was that Siddhartha's trumpet spent many days in Anjali's possession, until Mrinalini insisted he demand it back though he protested the kid might derive more use from it than he ever had. "Yeah," she sighed, "but you're not the one jumping from your skin when she starts her little concerts after lunch."

It was possibly even worse if Anjali acquired a possession legitimately her own. "My Papa got me," she would say, clutching a new and too-pink doll, its limbs already marked with crayon stains. "My Papa got me! What did your Papa get you?" – and for days there would be no escaping the fact that Mrinalini's Papa had, indeed, not got her anything – certainly not a doll you could decapitate at will.

"That kid," said Mrinalini after dinner, the night before Delhi's school admission season was officially declared open.

"Hmm? Anjali?"

"Yeah. You notice how she's changed?"

"Changed? Is she taller, or what?"

"Yeah, Sid. *Taller*."

"What?"

"You don't think she's becoming…"

"What?"

"You know... what's the word. Like a survivor. Hard, you know? Like her mother."

"Beena? I thought you liked her."

"Yeah, I like her. But she's hard. I mean... she's aspirational, right?"

"Fan-*cee*! Is it sociology night tonight?"

"Don't make fun of me."

"Never!"

"Fine, I'm going."

"No, Leenu, wait! Sorry... you were saying? You think she's got aspirations?"

"Yeah. You know... and her kid's getting them *from* her. Like all this grabby-ness... she wants Barbie bags and things all the time. A year ago she was more... innocent, you know? She cried when she heard that bhajan, remember?"

"Hmm..."

"And maybe it's our fault... *my* fault. Maybe that Sing-a-Song wasn't a good idea: it just fed them all these notions, you know?"

"Well, sweetheart, you can't not give someone an opportunity just because that'll make them want *more* opportunities."

"No, that's not what I mean. I just think... you can see she wants all the *wrong* things."

"Barbie bags?"

"Yeah."

"Hmm. Well. She'll probably grow out of them. Have you shortlisted some schools for them, by the way?"

"Well that's the *other* thing. Now, it seems they don't have her birth certificate, they'll have to go to the village to get it. And Chhote Lal's too scared to tell you and your mother because he thinks you'll shout at him, so he's telling me. So I told him... no listen, Sid! I told him, listen, that maybe your Dad could put in a word at a government school."

"Oh. You did? I thought we'd handle this ourselves, actually. I didn't really want them involved. Mama's already not so happy..."

"Yeah, but it'll be so much easier Sid. I mean, obviously. Otherwise we'll be running madly from school to school and have you even *seen* the competition? People save for years for the donation. In *lakhs*."

"Yeah. But you know I told them she's really bright and she'll make it. But if it's just going to be via some letter –"

"Not *just* some letter. Come on, she *is* bright.

And your Dad just has to make a teeny-tiny little recommendation, and the rest of it I'll do. I'll go with them, with the forms and everything. I'll meet the principal and everything."

"Okay. But Mama's not going to be happy."

"I know. Listen, Sid, I know this is a big pain for everyone. Maybe what we should do is," she curled a strand of his hair around her fingers, "maybe it's just better if we send them back, no? They can try next year, like you said."

"Oho, Leenu. Don't say that. We'll manage. I know you're keen…"

"No no, it's okay. I mean, I told you: maybe Delhi's not so good for her at all. Maybe she'll be *happier* in the village."

"Yeah." Siddhartha laughed.

"What?"

"Nobody's happier in the village, darling. That's why they're all here."

"Yeah, but…"

"Leenu, come on. You wanted this, fight for it. Let her *see* you fight. *That's* what we need in this country… not more doctors and lawyers. More people with spirit, you know?"

"I can't *make up* her birth certificate!"

"No… I don't mean that. I mean —"

"What?"

"I mean… look at your friend Jahanara, all these JNU types. She'll make this huge fuss about someone like Modi and, okay, fine, maybe he messed up in Gujarat with the riots, but you have to grant him, the man *loves* industry."

"Yeah?"

"And I mean people who are *industrious*. That's what I mean. And sure, people say he hates Muslims, but look at what's on the other side, look at what the Congress has done. And people like your friend, they're afraid of change, they're afraid they'll have to give up their canteens where they get their thirteen-rupee non-veg thalis and spend all day criticising the country that feeds them, they're afraid they'll have to stop crying for pity and start *working* —"

"Sid?"

"What? Thirteen rupees for a non-veg thali, can you believe that?"

"Sid, you're getting hyper."

He laughed. "Okay, sorry. I just… people like

184

her irritate me, you know? They act like they know everything."

"Okay, but what does that have to do with…"

"Just, sweetheart… I just don't like to have to *ask* for help unless I *have* to."

"Well in this case, then, I think you *have* to. Or we send her back. Honestly, Sid, I *really* don't mind."

He turned to her with an expression of such love she had to look away. "No, Leenu. I promised you, I know I did. You know I don't break promises, right? I'll talk to them."

"To who?"

"To Mama. I'll ask them for the letter. Happy?"

"Sure," said Mrinalini, biting her lip. "Yeah."

***

They sat on a wooden bench outside the Principal's office: Anjali in a new sweater and her best blue frock, Beena's hair neatly combed and her nose-ring gleaming. Even Mrinalini had chosen to wear her most straitlaced salwar kameez.

Siddhartha's father's recommendation had carried appreciable weight – the submission of forms had happened smoothly, and when Mrinalini asked to call on the Principal they were escorted to the door with great politeness and asked to wait only a few minutes, she would surely see them.

Anjali clung to her mother in palpitating excitement, from her nose running a perennial stream of mucus at which she would wipe with her sleeve split seconds before it reached her mouth, while Mrinalini stared, trying not to be disgusted, Beena said, "Look Anjali, look what a big school this is, do you see? Will you come to study here, Anjali?"

"Ya."

"What will you study, Anjali?"

"Everything!"

"Accha? Look how many teacher madams there are, look how many children will be in your class. You'll have so many friends, no, Anjali?"

"Ya."

"Then, you know who brought you to this big, nice school, Anjali?"

"Ya."

"Badi didi brought you. Isn't that right."

"Ya."

"Have you said thank you to badi didi?"

"Ya!"

"No, you haven't!"

Winter had brought no increase in conversation or eye-contact between them, so Mrinalini was surprised at this, at being invoked into the conversation with such a thing as a smile. "Oh," she said, almost abashed, "there's no need for thank you…" – and was grateful when the peon reappeared to escort them in.

"Clean your nose, Anju!" Beena wiped hurriedly with a tattered handkerchief, and then they were standing before the grey-haired Principal, seated across a table stacked from side to side with paper barricades, each held in place by rotund weights, of which the Principal seemed to have an impressive, and international, collection.

"Thank you for your time," said Mrinalini, adding "Ma'am" as further proof of gratitude.

"It's okay." She lifted her bottom off the chair, courteously. "Please sit."

"You must be very busy, at this time."

"Very true," she pushed her glasses up the rim of her nose with fingers that held a pen. "This *is* the busy season."

"And you must be getting so many requests. Thank you very much."

"Yes, dear, we do. Too, too many. But everybody wants to help, isn't it, and Mishra Sahib is such a senior officer. We are happy to help…"

"Oh but you must judge the child on her merit! She fully deserves it, I'm sure."

"Is that so?" They all turned to look at Anjali, sitting with her legs dangling off her mother's lap. "Well, you must have been observing her for a long time?"

"Yes, one year at least. I put her in a pre-school also, Sing-a-Song, maybe you've heard…?"

"There are so many these days."

"She's our maid's daughter, you see…"

"Yes. It is difficult for them, with no background, to keep the child educated. They must be very grateful for your help." She turned to Beena and shifted to Hindi. "They are helping you a lot."

"Yes," Beena whispered and smiled. As if, thought Mrinalini, the harsh ugliness of her voice through the garage door were an utter impossibility.

"Yes?"

"Yes, Madam."

"Well, dear," the Principal returned her eyes to Mrinalini, "please reassure Mishra Sahib, we will keep an eye on the application, there is no need…"

"But please, judge her on merit," said Mrinalini with a new urgency, "there are so many deserving children, we don't want to come in the way of any…"

"Of course not," the Principal frowned. "Is there any doubt in your mind?"

"Well…"

"Of course, we judge *every* child on their merit," she continued, seeming almost affronted. "Come," she looked at Anjali, "come here, child. Tell me your name."

Anjali buried her head in her mother's breasts. "Anju! Tell Madam your name!"

"It's Anjali," said Mrinalini, adding "Anjali? Let's hear your A-B-C!"

"Anjali?" The Principal's voice was more commanding, "Stand up and say A-B-C."

"Anju?" Beena tried to pull the child away from her, but Anjali clung to her neck and whimpered "Susu!"

"Shh!" said Beena, sharply, and got up to deposit her daughter on the floor, by the Principal's side. "Come on!"

With her eyes on the floor, Anjali began to sing, "A-B-*seedee*-E-F-*gee*," she paused and glanced up. The adults all smiled, and she continued a little louder, "H-I-J-K, ellemeno*pee*!"

Then she stopped, and turned into her mother's legs. They waited a moment. "Q?" Mrinalini suggested, "Q, R?" but Anjali wouldn't respond.

Embarrassed, Mrinalini laughed. "Sorry, Ma'am," she said to the Principal, who was shaking her head doesn't matter, "we see her every day, but we can hardly compare. And Mishra Sahib, he's not even in the country, you see."

"I see, dear. It's perfectly okay."

"She also knows her numbers."

"Is it? You," she said to Beena, "leave her and sit. Anjali? You know 1-2-3?"

As Beena moved away, Anjali seemed torn between a desire to cry and throw things. She didn't respond. Mrinalini frowned at Beena. With all her sulking, she could at *least* have made sure the kid was prepared. "Come on Anjali," she said, "*one…*"

Anjali looked up at her.

"*One…*" she repeated. "*Two.*"

"Very good! *Two…?*"

"*Three…*"

"Four?"

"*Leven.*"

"No! Say it properly!" And what was that stupid

190

Beena doing? Mrinalini turned to look at her, to urge her into action, but Beena's mouth had fallen open because Anjali, unwilling to unleash a flood of numbers at them had instead released a flow of pee. They watched, all three, spellbound by the trickle, as Anjali stared at nothing in particular, her eyes possessed of an almost mystic calm.

The Principal was first to react. She laughed. At the sound, as if shaken from sleep, Beena lunged towards Anjali, took her in her arms and ran out of the room. Mrinalini began to blabber her shame.

"I'm so sorry, so sorry! Your floor... I'm sorry, they wanted to send her back to the village, with her mother, but I *insisted*, I said, let her... your room! She's confused, this child, there's so much *difference*, they're so poor, how do they know the difference? This is terrible... with so much difference all around her!"

"It's okay, dear, okay," the Principal leaned back in her chair.

"She's *better* in her village, I was *telling* Siddhartha..."

"It's okay. You are right in one respect. Children develop a schizophrenic tendency, it is true, if they have so many role models."

"Exactly! But in the village, she will have a calm life. She will not feel always… *less*."

"Yes. Well, let me examine the case…"

"She *said* she wanted to go to the bathroom."

"I see. I will see her file, there is no problem."

"I'm sorry. I *myself* taught her *all* the A-B-C. But these people, they don't have *any* preparation!"

But already a woman had arrived with a mop and the Principal was scribbling something on a piece of paper as she said, "It's okay, dear. We have a lot of experience in these matters."

"Thank you."

"Welcome, welcome…"

Outside, she found Beena wearing a tense smile. "He didn't let us back in, didi," she gestured at the peon with her head. "Says we can't go."

"They'll call you if they want you, you don't understand or what?"

"He said…"

"It's okay," Mrinalini nodded at the peon and began walking away. "I spoke to the Principal. She'll keep an eye on the file."

"Anjali learnt all her A-B-C, 1-2-3… all waste." Beena tried to laugh as she said this, hurrying to catch up, and Mrinalini tried to smile in reply, but found she had to avert her eyes. "Arre, how waste?" she said abruptly. "She'll need it in life, won't she? Now come…" and began to walk a little faster back to the car.

If, by nightfall, anyone was excited by the thought of Anjali's shot at education, it was Siddhartha, who didn't even put on the news and wanted to know every detail of the day, and when he found that both Mrinalini and Beena looked away in vague reply, he asked for Anjali, bundled away into sleep, at which Mrinalini snapped. "Look, don't get them all worked up. Who knows? Maybe it'll not happen. The Principal said…"

"What? What'd she say?"

"Nothing! Just, she said they get a thousand requests and obviously they can't admit *everybody*, so you never know."

"Of course. But there's a pretty solid chance. I mean, I'll be surprised if…"

"Well, I won't."

"No?"

"No." Her stomach was a burning coil; she wanted to vomit it out. "I just got the impression. It's going to be difficult."

"Well, Mama said…"

"Uff, Sid! They're sitting so far away… there's people right here putting all kinds of pressure. She got half a dozen calls while I was *there*."

"No way."

"*Yes* way."

"Really?"

"Yes," she closed her eyes and said it again, "yes."

"Well. We'll just keep our fingers crossed then, I guess."

"Yeah."

"Where're you going?"

"To write! Whole day I spend running around…"

"Sure, of course," he smiled at her and reached for her hand but she had slipped away. The raucous caw of headlines followed her into the study, and she shut the door.

He didn't say much at dinner, which they ate in near silence, but later, when they had turned the lights off, he reached for her hand again and said, "Hey."

"Hey."

"Are you okay?"

"Okay?"

"You seem… I don't know. You seem worried."

"No." But it was too much now; she felt the tears gather and let them, until she had enough for a small sniffle.

"Hey!"

"What?"

"Are you crying?"

"No." She turned on her side, away from him, but immediately he had her encircled.

"Leenu? Darling? Tell me what happened?"

"Nothing. Oh Sid!" And now the tears really did flow and she wanted to tell him everything, "Oh Sid! I think I've done a terrible thing."

"Leenu! Don't be silly. God, I'm sorry… I never realised you cared so much!"

"But…"

"You *haven't* done anything terrible."

"No but… I just gave them all this *hope*, and now –"

"But Leenu, it'll work out. Why won't it?"

"Because I… I just…" But it was easier to cry than to speak as he held her, stroking her arm, kissing her hair, wiping the tears from her cheeks. It felt so good, this, with the frozen air of January pressing against them, huddling under the quilt.

"Hey," he said, "hey… listen" – she hiccupped and he laughed a little, kissing her again, she pushed herself into him – "listen, I know you don't like this subject, and maybe this isn't the time, but listen… it's just so clear to me how *good* you'd be as a… what a *great* mother you'd make – okay don't shout! – but I just know it, when I see you like this, how much you can care for some kid who's not even… I mean, most people would barely know her name, you know? Like me, I guess," he laughed again, "I'd never even have noticed her if you hadn't taken her in hand like you have, taken such care of her, been so *responsible*…"

"Oh Sid!"

"No really, listen. It's true, don't be modest. You *rock* at this. And you'd rock even louder if… I mean. What d'you say, hmm? What d'you think?"

Her tears dried. "You mean…?"

"Yeah. I mean… what d'you think? Say yes, come on."

He tightened his grip on her a little and she felt it again, the cold outside, the warmth within. It was impossible to say anything but,

"Okay."

"Really!" Siddhartha vaulted across her and took her face in his hands. "Really?"

"Maybe! Let me think about it: don't just impregnate me right *now*!"

"Yes, okay! Yes." His eyes shone in the dark; she couldn't bear it. Pulling herself into his chest, she mumbled "Hold me," and he obliged and she sighed and then she fell to a deep and dreamless sleep.

A few weeks later, they were informed by courteous phone-call that Anjali couldn't be, wouldn't be, hadn't been admitted – but they must, please, apply again next year. Only Siddhartha did them the courtesy of being surprised. Beena had long reverted to her sullen self, for which Chhote Lal was greatly apologetic; now he offered, himself, to send his wife and daughter back home. His ageing parents would appreciate the help, he said.

When Beena came to say goodbye, a week or so later, Mrinalini stood behind Siddhartha and let him do the talking. "We'll try again next year, don't worry," he said, bending to pat Anjali's head. "And don't forget what to do if a ghost comes!" At this, he chuckled to himself and Anjali seemed to smile and Mrinalini said, "Oh wait!" and she walked across to her wallet and took out a thousand rupees and pressed them into Beena's reluctant hand. "You *must* remember to give her coconut water every day!"

Beena nodded and Siddhartha turned to look at his wife and saw that she was rubbing at her eyes, so he dismissed them quickly, not wanting anything to trouble Mrinalini in her potentially pregnant state.

So he knew she was worried, and why should she not be? Mrinalini *was* sad. For days after they left, she nurtured a tiny, perfect core of sadness for Beena and Anjali's fate; it stung at the most unexpected moments – at the sight of a particularly cheerful urchin, or at those social service ads that feature dark girls with white teeth.

Jahanara sent her a Facebook invitation to something called Queer Open Mic; Brajeshwar came down to tell them both of a panel discussion he was part of. It was titled "I Cannot Say Just What I Mean: The Dangers of Writing in New India".

Siddhartha said it would be rude not to go, so they went. Afterwards, she told him about Jahanara's thing. He laughed and said, sure, if you want. Will it all be weird poetry, but?

That night, Mrinalini clicked 'Maybe' on the invite and closed the window.

In sum: Mrinalini Singh waited for all her little atoms to do their bit, to settle in some grid, and pick up speed. When, eventually, the feeling passed, Mrinalini was sitting at her desk, staring at the blank first page of a new word document titled Novel-2. With a surge of inspiration, she closed it. Then, she opened the last draft of her first book. All it needed, she realised, was a sub-plot on the doomed aspirations of a young maid's toddling child.

Acknowledgements

There are, no doubt, writers who become whirlwinds of creative genius as they work, an inspiration to behold. Myself, I prefer the grumpy-needy method. When I'm not worrying about how people aren't giving me enough space, I worry about drifting all alone in a black void. Every once in a while, I produce a draft and pounce upon the unsuspecting with it.

Even so, a lot of people were very nice to me as I wrote this book. Some read a draft (some read more than one, and may god shower them with jewels). Some published extracts from a work that only the cheeriest optimist could, at that point, have called either a novel or in progress. Some played scrabble. Some asked, in a kindly way, about the book's progress. Some poured whisky.

Thank you: Anita Abraham, Ayushi Saxena, Fatma and Tahseen Alam, Gayatri Sharma, Mallika Ghosh, Mayur Suresh, Namita Malhotra, Polly Hazarika, Priya Gangwani, Ruchika Negi and Amit Mahanti, Sarita and Anmol Vellani, Subasri Krishnan and Jawahar Raja, Swati Mitra, Trisha Gupta.

Thank you Anita Roy, of Zubaan, and R. Sivapriya, of Penguin.

My deepest thanks to my whole family for their grace and support. And to Shahrukh, for generously giving me all her opinions, and for making me laugh.

About Zubaan

Zubaan is an independent feminist publishing house based in New Delhi with a strong academic and general list. It was set up as an imprint of India's first feminist publishing house, Kali for Women, and carries forward Kali's tradition of publishing world quality books to high editorial and production standards. Zubaan means tongue, voice, language, speech in Hindustani. Zubaan is a non-profit publisher, working in the areas of the humanities, social sciences, as well as in fiction, general non-fiction, and books for children and young adults under its Young Zubaan imprint.

About the Zubaan-Penguin joint list

The Zubaan-Penguin joint list was established in 2005. Under this collaborative arrangement the two publishing houses together produce a list of distinctive and exceptional fiction and non-fiction writing mostly by women writers with a special focus on gender. Books published under this imprint include *The Circle of Karma* by Kunzang Choden, *Lunatic in My Head* by Anjum Hasan, *Seeing Like a Feminist* by Nivedita Menon and *The Missing Queen* by Samhita Arni. You can visit both our websites to view the complete list: www.zubaanbooks.com; www.penguinbooksindia.com